Her Stubborn Cowboy

Cameron Hart

Published by Cameron Hart, 2024.

HER STUBBORN COWBOY

First edition. February 23, 2024.

ISBN: 979-8224301805

Written by Cameron Hart.

Want a free book?

Sign up for my newsletter[1] and get your free copy of Chasing Stacy!

One look at the stunning waitress carrying the weight of the world on her shoulders, and I'm a goner. I wasn't looking for a sweet little thing with auburn hair and more baggage than I can fit on the back of my bike, but there's no going back now. She's mine. I'll prove to her I'm more than capable of handling her past and making her feel safe again.

Connect with me!

Check out my website, cameronhart.net[2], for sneak previews on my latest projects.

Follow me on social media:

Facebook Page - facebook.com/cameronhartauthor
   Instagram - instagram.com/cameron.hart.author
   TikTok - tiktok.com/@author.cameron.hart
   Goodreads - goodreads.com/16081533.Cameron_Hart
   Bookbub - bookbub.com/authors/cameron-hart

Chapter 1

Jade

"Nice of you to come back for the funeral," the snippy, nosy Uber driver says, her words dripping with sarcasm. I should expect nothing less in this small Texas town. I was thoroughly surprised to even find an Uber driver who would take me all the way out here to the ranch, but it turns out she lives here too. Great.

"Yes, well, he is my father. *Was* my father," I correct myself. "Or, well, I guess he still is. But just...dead. He's dead." I finish, awkwardly. This shuts the judgmental middle-aged woman up. Good. She can keep her passive-aggressive remarks to her own damn self.

The rest of the drive is mercifully silent. I watch the congestion of the airport give way to long stretches of highway. Traffic thins out as we follow a winding path towards my childhood home, Rivera Ranch.

I haven't been back here since I left for Denver right after I turned eighteen, nearly four years ago. The whole town, including Ms. Snarky Uber Driver, thinks I'm an ungrateful little swine who ran away as soon as I got a chance. They're not wrong; at least about the running away part. It's the ungrateful part that we can never seem to see eye to eye on.

No one knew my daddy like I did. The whole town loves him. *Loved* him. Aw, hell, they still love him.

Good ol' Jim Rivera was always willing to lend a hand. The life of the party. A family man to boot, even after his wife skipped out on him and his daughter did the same ten years later. He's good lookin' too, wonder why he never remarried?

Yes, I know all about the image Dad liked to keep up around town. The shit part about being his only family is that no one would believe me if I told them otherwise. No one *did* believe me. I learned my lesson early on and kept my mouth shut, my head down, and got away as soon as I was legally able.

It's not that I didn't love my dad; I did. And I know down to my very core that he loved me too, the best way he knew how. But that doesn't excuse the pain he caused, the lies he told, the scars he left behind.

I've come to terms with my relationship with my father. Or, at least, I had up until I got a call three days ago informing me that my dad met an untimely death when he fell from the loft of the barn. A tide of emotion swells up inside of me just remembering that call. It brought me to my knees. Literally. I had just returned to my apartment after the worst day ever when I got the news. How could one day be so utterly fucked up?

I swallow down tears thinking about the life I left back in Denver. Or, more accurately, the life I no longer have in Denver. There's nothing left for me there. Even more heartbreaking is the fact that there's really nothing left for me here, either. Just a town full of people who idolize my father and think they know me.

"This is it," my Uber driver tells me, breaking me out of my little pity party. She says it all snarkily like I wouldn't remember what my house looked like. "See you at the funeral tomorrow."

"Thanks," I mumble half-heartedly. She gives me some strong side-eye, the way only a true Southerner can, and pops the trunk so I can grab my bags.

The crunch of gravel under the tires slowly fades, and soon it's just me and my childhood home. I was so busy the last few days packing up everything I could and making funeral arrangements over the phone that I didn't have time to stop and imagine what it would actually be like to be standing here again.

Grief hits me so swiftly and powerfully I have to gasp for my next breath of air. It's the same. Peeling paint, porch swing, and all. Sorrow, rage, remorse, and profound loneliness churn deep inside of me and squeeze my heart with such pain and intensity, I might just cave in on myself and cease to exist.

I feel as though my body is made of lead, but I somehow manage to drag one foot in front of the other until I reach the front door. The screen door still has a tear in the top left corner, and the spare key is still tucked under the doormat.

With a final cleansing breath, I turn the key and push the door open, taking my first step inside. It's truly like I never left. I'm expecting my dad to come around the corner and either sweep me up in a hug or yell at me about not going to the grocery store even though he never told me I needed to. I could never tell with him, which made me cautious to trust anything good in my life. I'm still always waiting for the other shoe to drop, which is probably why I've never had a real relationship, boyfriend, friend, or otherwise.

Shaking those thoughts from my head, I continue on inside, dragging my suitcases behind me. I should probably eat dinner and take a shower, but both of those things require energy I no longer have.

I look at the clock on the microwave and see it's half past eight in the evening. It's as good a time as any to go to bed. I think I deserve it after the shit-tastic week I've had. I don't even turn on any lights as I make my way upstairs to where the bedrooms are. The main floor of the house is used by the ranch hands for meals and relaxing at the end of the day. Which reminds me that I have to go talk to everyone and check out the property and file for a life insurance claim and...

Tomorrow. I'll deal with it all tomorrow. The funeral is at eleven, which leaves plenty of time to sort through all of the things I'm too young and inexperienced to know how to do, like evaluate an estate and balance the books. On the plus side, it'll keep me busy.

But for now...sleep. I collapse on my bed in my old room, refusing to acknowledge the weird ache in my gut that flared up as soon as I walked in and saw everything exactly how I left it - unmade bed and all. So the sheets haven't been changed in four years. Another thing I'll deal with tomorrow. At this point, I'm just happy to be sleeping on a bed.

Without another thought to the state of the bed or the state of affairs I have to work through come sunrise, I pull the blankets up and sleep like the dead. No pun intended.

***

I should have prepared a eulogy. Here we are, twenty-five minutes into the funeral, and it hits me that I don't even know what to say about my dad, at least not to these people. The preacher gave a short message and then asked if anyone had any words they wanted to say to remember Jim Rivera.

Of course, plenty of people went to the pulpit and said their peace. *Jim mended my fence, Jim visited me in the hospital, Jim had a smile for everyone. He had a successful ranch all while raising his daughter.*

Yeah, that one earned me a few glares. *Fuck you guys, too.* I didn't say that, but God did I want to. For some reason, all these people saying nice things about my daddy is getting me all agitated. Several times I've had to literally bite my tongue from screaming, *You didn't know him"* *"!at all*

Instead, I nod and smile politely in all the right places. I do muster up some tears, but only out of frustration. The town is mourning someone who didn't really exist.

Finally, the preacher nods his head in my direction, indicating it's my turn to wrap things up with a heartfelt speech to send my dad off into the great beyond and at the same time comfort those he left behind.

Great. This totally won't be a shit show.

I slowly make my way to the pulpit and grip the sides with shaking hands. I swear my heart is going to crack a rib or three with how hard it's pounding right now. I can't look anyone in the eye, so I skim over their heads, hoping they won't notice the difference. It's not like anyone here has looked at me with anything but thinly veiled disdain since my arrival. This is Texas, however, so their disapproval is all wrapped up in *bless your little heart!*

I blow out a shallow breath and dig up words from the very core of me. I just have to get through this and then the burial, where thankfully I won't have to say anything.

"Thank y'all for the kind words. My daddy would have loved knowing that you thought so highly of him." Well, that much at least is true. "He lived and breathed this town, and he sure was proud to call it home for his entire life." I wince at the direction this little speech is taking, no doubt drawing attention to how I ran away from here as soon as I got the chance. "Jim Rivera had a big heart and thought of y'all as his family, and I know you viewed him the same way. Thanks for loving my daddy."

My voice catches on my last words, actual tears of grief and loss clogging my throat. The truth of it is, they loved my dad in a way I couldn't. They got the best parts of him, and that's what they'll remember.

The preacher pats my shoulder and walks me down the aisle of the little chapel and outside to where the graveyard is conveniently located in the back. Everyone follows my lead until we're crowded around a hole in the ground, waiting for the coffin to be lowered six feet deep.

I'm surrounded by sniffles and some outright crying, while I stand stoic as ever, once my little outburst of emotion passed.

"As much as it has pleased Almighty God of his great mercy to take unto himself the soul of our dear brother here departed, we, therefore, commit his body to the ground; earth to earth, ashes to ashes, dust to dust..." the preacher drones on. I tune out until I hear, "Amen."

He's finally done reading from the Book of Common Prayer and one by one people step forward to toss a handful of dirt on the lowered coffin. It's like a scene from a movie, but it's playing out in real life. Still, I'm detached. Confused. Hurting. Angry. I feel like I'm going crazy, and yet I feel numb at the same time. There's no doubt about it; grief is a bitch.

Half an hour later, I'm in the church basement with a plate full of food, though I have no idea where it came from. I vaguely remember someone handing me a plate with a meatball on it, and then more food was piled on, and more, and now the dang thing is buckling under the weight of uneaten, unappetizing food.

All around me I hear story after story of the soft-hearted Jim, the poor Jim who died without his wife or his daughter by his side, the funny, outgoing Jim who always had a good story and a great joke.

It's too much. All of it. The walls start pressing in around me and I have the overriding need to get the fuck out of here. I set my plate down before it falls from my suddenly sweaty hands, and beeline towards the stairs that lead directly outside.

Three stairs to freedom, two, one...

I open the door and run smack into a brick wall. I feel a solid warmth wrapping its way around my shoulders and back, and then a low, gravelly voice rumbles up from the chest—not brick wall—that I'm currently pressed against.

"Woah there, darlin', are you okay?"

I peer up into soft, warm brown eyes that crinkle ever so slightly at the edges when the man gives me a gentle smile. I recognize the handsome face staring back at me, though I can't quite put it together. Something about his familiarity, his cypress and rain smell, the way his eyes hold only kindness without even a hint of judgment, has me bursting into tears.

"I've got you, sweetheart, I've got you. Let it all out now, it's okay," he murmurs, tucking my head under his chin while I snot and cry all over his shirt. I should feel embarrassed, but honestly, I'm so overwhelmed with everything else, I don't have the capacity for even one more emotion.

The absolutely crazy thing is, each soft-spoken word and comforting stroke of his hand on my back calms me down more and more. I didn't think anything could anchor me in this flood of emotion, but here I am, finding steady ground in the arms of a stranger.

He seems to sense when I'm all cried out and loosens his hold on me so he can lead me the rest of the way outside. I can't help the heat that courses through my body when he keeps one hand at the small of my back.

When we're finally to the edge of the little field in front of the chapel, the stranger with the kind eyes turns and looks me over as if inspecting me for damage. It's then I realize he's no stranger.

"Noah?" I squeak out, my voice still not fully recovered from my little outburst.

"I'm surprised you remembered me."

I wince at his words, thinking it's another dig at me being gone for so long, but when I look at him, he's got no bite or bitterness in his features.

"Of course I remember you," I say all too quickly. I can feel my cheeks turning pink at my confession. My daddy hired Noah as the foreman of the ranch my senior year of high school. He was stunning back then, all brawn and muscle and tanned skin, and he's even more gorgeous now, from what I can tell. A little older, a few grey hairs at his temples that stand out against his otherwise dark, full head of hair, more lines around his face, but all of that only serves to make him look distinguished. Experienced. The very definition of ruggedly handsome. "I mean, um, because you work at the ranch," I'm quick to add.

Noah gives me an amused smile. "That's right," he drawls. "Goin' on four years now."

"I'm Jade," I blurt out stupidly. I'd like to blame it on the stress of the funeral, but that charm right there is all me.

"I know," he grins at me. "Can I give you a ride? I get the sense you're about as ready to be out of here as I am. Oh, uh, no offense," he adds, sheepishly.

"Absolutely none taken," I chuckle. "You're right. I'm very much over this whole scene, though I should probably stick around to clean everything up, right?"

"Nah. What would all these meddling church biddies do with themselves if they didn't have a mess to attend to?" He winks, and a soft laugh bubbles up from my chest. I feel something shift in me, a weight lifting off my chest, just enough to get a full breath in.

"In that case, yes. I'd love to get the hell out of here."

Chapter 2

Noah

I watch Jade walk up to the main house and bite back a groan. My thoughts towards her are shameful and so very inappropriate, especially considering we just came from her father's funeral for fuck's sake.

And yet, I can't help but stare at her ass in that black dress of hers. It's not revealing or even very tight. It's modest, in fact. But her curves fill it out quite nicely. I discreetly adjust my hardening cock as I remember those soft curves pressed up against the solid muscles of my chest and torso. Christ, I shouldn't be thinking of her that way, and certainly not while she's grieving.

Plus, there's the fact that she's sixteen years my junior and now technically my boss. Neither of those facts helps my painful state of arousal.

It's more than lust though. Holding her small, curvy body as she shook from her sobs triggered something deep inside of me. Some long-dormant protective urge came crawling out, and soft words of comfort poured from my lips. I'm a cowboy through and through, tough, weathered, and foul-mouthed to boot. Never have I spoken so gently to another living soul, but with Jade, it came so naturally.

Of course I remember the fiery redhead from when I was first hired on nearly four years ago. She was too young for me to appreciate her the way I do now, but there's no mistaking her wild hair, the stubborn spark in her clear green eyes, and her elusive smile. She's beautiful and untamed.

And I'm just the cowboy to rope her in.

Stop it, you goddamn pervert, I chastise myself. There's no way she'd go for an old man like me, and to be honest, I don't think I have it in me to hand my heart over only to get it stomped on again.

Thoughts of my ex have my hard on deflating in no time. I suppose I better catch up on the chores I missed after taking time off to attend the funeral.

Try as I might to throw my mind and body into the satisfying and grueling work of keeping up the ranch and overseeing the other ranch hands, my thoughts keep drifting back to Jade.

Specifically, I replay her closing words she spoke about her father. Or, rather, about the town. Never once did she mention how much he meant to her or share a fond memory much like the others who stood up there and reminisced over Jim Rivera. Something about that unsettles me.

I figured their relationship was strained, considering Jade left right after graduating high school and never came back for a visit. I hear the bullshit people say around town about her - ungrateful, flakey, self-serving. I don't believe any of it, and I've told more than one person that it's none of their damn business.

I don't blame them for ignoring me, though, what with Jim talking about Jade all the time to anyone who would listen. It was clear he was proud of her and the work she was doing in Denver. But every once in a while, his praise and adoration for his daughter felt hollow. Disingenuous, even. From what I gathered, she didn't go to college, but instead got a job right out of high school at a PR agency and worked her way up from the bottom over the last few years.

Which is another reason why Jade and I are all wrong for each other. She high-tailed it far away from the ranch and ran straight to the city. I don't begrudge her that at all, it just shows me what her priorities are. Fast-paced, high stakes, and having an exciting, lavish life. All of those things are about as far away from my idea of a good life as possible. I learned my lesson about trying to convince a city girl to settle down with me.

My ex wanted money, success, and the hustle of the city. Or at the very least a house in the 'burbs within five minutes of a Starbucks. She was never satisfied with my dream to own my own ranch one day. It was never enough for her. *I* was never enough for her. It took me catching her in bed with her boss to finally realize we would never work out.

That was over eight years ago. Since then, I've kept my head down, worked hard, and stored every penny in the bank. I've had enough money to buy my own land and build a small ranch for some time now, what with my savings and inheritance money I received a few years ago when my grandfather died. But without anyone to share it with, my dream seems lonely and unsatisfying. I figured I might as well keep saving and working at Rivera Ranch. I'm not sure what I'm waiting for, exactly, but something stirs inside of me as Jade's lovely face and fierce eyes pop into my head.

I shake away the ridiculous idea of running a ranch with Jade by my side and our kids playing and making messes and memories around the property.

Shit. Kids? You've lost it, Noah.

With a cleansing breath and a roll of my shoulders in an attempt to relieve some of the tension, I start to make the rounds to check on the various projects and the ranch hands working on them. With a nod and a grunt of approval for each one, I dismiss them for the day. The five of us workers all made it out to the funeral, and I know the mixture of loss, uncertainty of the future, and working twice as hard to catch up on chores has taken a toll.

The four ranch hands I'm in charge of, Jacob, Isaiah, Cory, and Zane, all make their way to their cabins. Jacob and Isaiah, the twins, share a cabin, and I get a cabin to myself as the foreman. There's also an empty cabin for the cook we haven't replaced yet. Cory and Zane live at home with their wives and kids.

After a shower, a bowl of warmed up chili, and a beer, I start to get restless. I should be exhausted, but my mind is racing. The buzz I feel isn't from the single beer I had, but rather from the unshakable need to check on Jade. As hard as today was for me, it was a thousand times worse for her, despite whatever complicated relationship she had with her father.

Before I can overthink it, I'm up and out of my favorite oversized chair by the fireplace and making my way towards the main house. When I'm a few yards away, I see Jade curled up on the porch swing in nothing but a baggy t-shirt and pajama shorts. She has a glass of whiskey on the side table next to her, and surprisingly, she's puffing away at a cigarette.

I'm only a few feet away from her, standing at the bottom of the stairs leading up to the porch, but she's so lost in thought she doesn't even notice me. It allows me to drink in her smooth skin, high cheekbones, delicate, kissable lips, and messy, beautiful red hair. My hands itch to tangle themselves in those crazy locks and tilt her head back so I can suck on her neck.

Fuck, get it together, man.

I scramble for something to say, some way to draw her attention towards me, even though I'm not sure if I can handle it. Instead of saying something charming or comforting, I say the first thing that comes to mind.

"Those things will kill you, ya know," I blurt out, referring to the cigarette in her hand. Apparently, I used up all of my gentle words on her earlier.

Jade jumps about ten feet in the air and slaps her free hand over her chest to calm her heart down.

"Sorry," I say, stepping up to the porch with my hands out in surrender to show her I'm no threat. "Didn't mean to startle you. Just wanted to check-in and see how you're doing."

Jade gives me a small smile, and if I'm not mistaken, she even blushes a little. It's hard to tell with the sun setting. Might just be a trick of the light, but I'd like to think she's just as affected by me as I am by her.

"Oh," she says once she's got her breathing under control. "That's mighty kind of you," she says in that Texas twang of hers that I like so much. It makes me unreasonably happy that she never lost it even while she was away. Jade scoots over and pats the seat next to her in a silent invitation. One that I gladly accept.

The porch swing creaks under my weight, and for a second I think it might not hold the both of us. Jade seems to read my thoughts.

"Don't worry, this old swing is as sturdy and stubborn as everything else around this ranch," she says, her lips tilting up in a small, wistful smile.

"That right?"

She nods her head and takes a sip of her whiskey, though she winces as she swallows. I can't help but stare at the motion in her throat.

"Is that what I am, too? Sturdy and stubborn?" I ask, trying and failing to tear my eyes away from her slender neck and images of marking her creamy skin by sinking my teeth into her tender flesh and then kissing away the sting. Jesus, I don't think I've ever been this out of control over a woman before.

Jade eyes me up and down and gives a decisive nod of her head. "It's not a bad thing. Sturdy is good. Stable. Dependable. All admirable qualities."

"And stubborn?"

She grins, the beautiful way it lights up her face making me dizzy. "That can be good too, as long as you're stubborn about the right things."

"Oh? And what are the right things?" I ask, returning her grin.

"Isn't part of the fun finding that out on your own?"

I chuckle at her response and take the cigarette from her hand, tapping it on the railing of the porch to get rid of the ashes before handing it back to her. I don't want them falling on her lap and burning her, after all. There's that protective side coming out again, wanting to do anything and everything to look after her.

Jade takes the cigarette but ends up tossing it into the half-finished glass of whiskey. "I'm not much of a drinker, and I never smoke. I found the whiskey and cigarettes in the kitchen and just felt...I don't know. Like I'd be close to him? Understand him? It's dumb. I'm not even sure what I'm doing." She shrugs, looking off into the distance again. I resist the urge to pull her into my arms and opt instead to reach deep down inside of me again to try and muster up more words of comfort.

"It's not dumb. It makes sense you'd want to remember him after being away for so long." I know I said the wrong thing when she winces and leans away from me. Dammit, I'm no good at this shit. Without thinking about it, I reach out and rest my hand on her knee. "Hey, I didn't mean it like that. I'm sure you had your reasons for leaving, and it's no one's business but yours," I say softly, trying to recover.

Jade stares at my hand but doesn't shy away from my touch. In fact, she seems to relax a bit, though she doesn't respond.

"How's life in the city anyway? You live in Denver now, right?" I ask.

Her face pales, but she recovers quickly enough to make me doubt I saw anything at all. "Uh, yeah, yeah, it's fine," she answers hurriedly before changing the subject. "How about the ranch? Are you still liking it here? As your new boss, your job satisfaction is my number one priority," she winks at me, though I can tell she's tense about whatever is going on in her life back in Denver. I tell myself it's not my problem, but I want her to trust me enough to tell me all of her secrets. Fuck, I feel myself getting all tangled up in this woman, but I'm powerless to stop it.

Clearly, she's uncomfortable talking about herself, so I let her have this out. "The ranch is good. It's hard work, but it's honest. I've never wanted to do anything else with my life," I tell her truthfully.

Jade asks me more about the day-to-day operations, and I tell her everything she wants to know. She scoots closer and closer, till she's leaning against my shoulder. I can tell it's an involuntary movement, just something that seems natural. Just like how natural it is for me to remove my hand from her knee so I can wrap my arm around her shoulders. She cuddles up into my side as if we've done this every single night for years. I won't lie, it feels good. Too damn good.

I ramble on about the ranch, telling her stories about some of the shenanigans the other ranch hands have pulled. Not me, of course. I'm too mature to partake in such things. Mostly.

Soon I feel her little body go limp as she presses her weight into my side. I pull her close and breathe in her peaches and cream scent. We stay like that for a while, me holding her while she sleeps. I feel a peace wash over me, like nothing I've ever experienced before.

Shoving that thought and the unwelcomed, confusing emotions it triggers aside, I try nudging Jade. I don't really want her to leave my side, but I also can't afford to get even more wrapped up in her. When she doesn't budge even an inch, I have to chuckle. The woman is a heavy sleeper. Or maybe she's just worn out after the last few days.

Either way, I decide she needs to be tucked into bed, even if I have to do it myself. My chest gets tight as I lift her up into my arms, watching her curl up into me and bury her head in between my neck and shoulder.

I carry her into the house, shutting the door lightly with my foot. I've only been upstairs a few times when I needed to talk to Jim in his office. I know the bedrooms are up there, so that's where I head.

I'm not sure how I know, but hers is the second door on the left, I'm sure of it. When I nudge the door open, I see that I'm right. The room looks like it was decorated by a sixteen-year-old girl, which I suppose makes sense. It's a bit chaotic, colorful, and sweet. Just like Jade.

The sheets smell fresh like she did laundry as soon as I dropped her off earlier in the day. The thought of her cleaning up and doing house chores after getting back from her dad's funeral doesn't sit right with me. I'll have to stop by tomorrow morning and see if there's anything else she needs done around the house. God knows Jade has enough on her plate figuring out stuff with the ranch. I'll try to help her out there as much as possible too.

I reluctantly lay her down on the bed once I've pulled the blankets back. She murmurs something in her sleep and then curls up in a little ball. She looks so tiny and vulnerable. It's all I can do not to crawl into bed with her and cover her with my body, my strength, my warmth. But that's not my place. I'll settle for taking care of her from a distance.

Despite my little pep talk, I find myself tucking the blankets around her and pressing my lips to her forehead as if she's mine to care for. I don't like how hard it is for me to pull away from her. I especially don't like the little stab of pain deep in my gut as I turn and walk away. My steps are heavy and slow like I'm trudging through mud.

I allow myself one last look over my shoulder at her delicate sleeping form, and then I force myself to shut her door and walk away. What is this woman doing to me?

Chapter 3

The first thing I notice when I wake up is that I smell like Noah; rain and cypress. I remember him interrupting my little pity party on the porch last night and talking to me about the ranch.

I somehow ended up tucked into his side with his strong, warm, comforting arm wrapped around my shoulders. It didn't feel awkward or like I was crossing boundaries, even though I probably was. No, it felt natural. So natural, in fact, that I didn't even think twice about getting cozy with the handsome older man with kind, brown eyes.

I breathe in more of his scent and remember his low, gravelly voice lulling me to sleep. My eyes snap open with that realization. He must have carried me up here and tucked me in. My face flushes with embarrassment, but my tummy erupts with butterflies at the thought of him taking care of me. Not that I need a man to take care of me. But still, it was a nice gesture. I can't recall a time in my life anyone has watched over me like that.

Rolling over, I grab my phone to check the time. My stomach drops when I see I have six missed calls from my boss back in Denver. Well, my *former* boss, that is. God, what a fucking mess. All of it. Everything. My dad, my job, the heinous way I was fired, and the subsequent fallout. I can't think about it anymore or else I might just break. And I don't have time to break. Not until I get my shit together and figure out what to do with the disaster my life has become.

I stretch and work out the kinks in my limbs and back before planting my feet on the solid ground. It's just after eight in the morning, which means I've already missed breakfast with the workers. Usually, they are up and at 'em by five or so.

It's probably for the best. I need to get a better idea of how my dad was taking care of the ranch. I couldn't help but notice some things that could use fixing up when I was surveying the property from my seat on the porch last night. The cattle barn looked worse for wear, the fence along the north side of the property line has a few posts that need replacing soon, and don't even get me started on the main house.

The mental list of repairs is getting longer and longer, and so is the to-do list. I'm equal parts overwhelmed and thankful for things that will keep me busy and distracted, especially if Adam, ex-asshole-creeper-boss, is trying to get ahold of me.

I shake the thoughts of my former boss away and get dressed. I should probably shower, but I find I don't want to wash Noah's scent off of me. Pathetic, I know. Getting involved with the much older, much hotter, much more experienced man is totally out of the question, no matter how much my body wants to.

It's a new feeling for me. Not just being comfortable in a near stranger's presence, but responding to him the way I do. I'd be lying if I said having his hand on my knee didn't cause my lady parts to throb in a new and exciting way. I have pretty much zero experience with men, which is another reason Noah and I would never work. I'm sure he wants someone his own age who knows how to please him, or at the very least, someone who has seen a dick before.

Yes, at twenty-one, I'm still a virgin. I'm not ashamed of it or anything, but it's not exactly something I go advertising. Though I'm sure Noah would figure it out just from one kiss. He would probably taste my fumbling inexperience and walk away from me.

Not that we'll be kissing, of course.

Books. I need to check the books and finances. Yes, this will give me purpose and keep my mind occupied and focused on something other than the sexy cowboy and the way he makes me feel both safe and turned on at the same time. I couldn't possibly look at budgets and spreadsheets while also imagining what he looks like underneath his plaid shirt and form-fitting Levi's. Right? Right.

I slide on a pair of fuzzy socks and make my way into my dad's office. It's strange being in here. I keep expecting him to show up and yell at me to get the hell out of his space. Father didn't like me to be in here for whatever reason. Which makes my task harder. I don't know anything about how he ran the ranch, but I suppose none of that matters now. It's up to me to figure it out. I'm up for the challenge, though. Everything I've done so far in life has been hard-earned, and this will be no different.

Before I know it, I'm lost in tax forms and folders of crumpled, unorganized receipts. I have twelve tabs open on the browser on my computer, each one outlining the basics of balancing checkbooks, or how to run Turbo Tax software, or how to do payroll for a small business. It seems like every new thing I research and every new file I find only raises more questions.

I need a list. First things first. Payroll. I need the ranch hands now more than ever, so they need to get paid. Then, I'll look up dad's life insurance policy and talk to the bank. After that, I'll balance the books, figure out operating costs, and what our profit margins look like. When I've gathered all of that information, I can call Dad's lawyer and see what we can do about selling the ranch.

My gut twists at that thought. Of course, I want to sell the ranch. That was my plan ever since I got the call about my dad's death. I mean, I hadn't really thought it all out in detail or anything like that, but in the back of my head, I knew I'd never officially move back here. The only other option then is to sell. I'll use the money to start over and find a home somewhere else.

Noah's dark, slightly greying hair, warm smile, and bright, twinkling brown eyes pop into my head. Why do I associate him and the way it felt to be in his arms with the word home?

There's no time to think about all that. I have payroll to do and budgets to balance.

Three hours later, I have a crick in my neck and a rock sitting heavy in my stomach. I'm no accountant, but even I can see we're struggling. After cutting checks to the five workers on the ranch, we barely have enough to pay property taxes, let alone do repairs, hire a cook, or invest anything back into the ranch to keep it growing, or hell, just keep it afloat.

"Fuck," I mutter to myself as I run my hands through my tangled hair for the thousandth time today. My mind is running in circles trying to think of some magical solution. I go over the spreadsheets and checkbook again, hoping I just missed something. A revenue stream I overlooked. An investment that's going to pay off soon. An expense we no longer have. But once again, I come to the same conclusion.

We're screwed.

The room starts to spin, and I realize I haven't eaten anything or had anything to drink all day, and it's almost two in the afternoon. That coupled with the stress of the last week is starting to get to me.

After several glasses of water and a sandwich, I decide to go visit my horse. That is if she's still here. She's not really *mine*, per se, but she was my favorite. Stella. We got her when I was ten. She birthed several foals, most of which we sold. She'd be too old to have any more at this point, and the thought of my dad getting rid of her has me running out to the stables.

I'm breathless by the time I reach my destination, but I manage a sigh of relief when I see Stella. I reach my hand out and let her nuzzle me, getting used to me again. After a few minutes, I step into her stall and begin brushing her hair. It's something that has always calmed me.

Memories come flooding back of escaping out here when my dad was in one of his moods. I spent hours out here talking to Stella and running a brush through her mane before saddling her up and taking a ride. I'd pretend I was running away. Sometimes I'd camp out all night in the treehouse I built one summer.

Some small part of me always hoped my dad would come out and find me and apologize for losing his temper, but he never did. He never asked where I went, or even seemed to notice when I was gone. Unless, of course, we were supposed to be somewhere in public or he needed me to be by his side for some business deal to make him look like the perfect single dad.

Shit, this isn't any better than being cooped up in the office. My head is spinning, but not from numbers and spreadsheets. It's from the uncomfortable feeling of thinking ill of the dead. I need fresh air. And a new to-do list.

It's been years since I've ridden, but I saddle up Stella in no time, my muscle memory kicking in and going through the motions even if my mind isn't fully present.

Suddenly, the air changes. My back is to the door of the stables, but somehow I just know. It's him. *Noah*. I feel his calming, peaceful presence wash over me.

"I was wondering if I'd see you today," he says in his deep, soothing voice.

"Yup, I'm afraid you're stuck with me for a bit. At least until I figure out...all of this," I gesture vaguely around me.

He nods in understanding, his captivating eyes never leaving me. I feel vulnerable under his concentrated gaze like he's trying to peel back all of my layers and see into the very core of who I am. The thing is, I don't even know who I am anymore. If he figures it out, I'd like him to inform me right away.

"I always do my best thinking while riding," he says after clearing his throat and looking away from me. As unsettled as I was by his intense scrutiny of me, I feel cold and lonely without it.

I ignore that thought and focus on tightening the straps on the saddle. "Yeah. It's been a while for me, but I think the fresh air will do me some good. Going over the books left me with a headache."

He turns his head towards me, and I see a flash of concern cover his stubbled, handsome face. "Mind if I join you?" He finally says.

I'm not sure if I can take more alone time with him without spontaneously combusting, but I also can't stand the thought of riding alone now that he's offered to come with me. I'm so fucked. Noah is messing with my head at a time that I can't even figure out up from down. As crazy as it sounds, however, he feels like the only stable thing in my life at the moment.

"Sure, company would be nice." I give him a small smile, which he returns. We stare at each other for a beat too long. I feel a blush creeping up into my cheeks, so I turn away and fiddle with something on the saddle.

A few minutes later, Noah has Otis saddled up and we're taking off towards the east end of the ranch, where a small stream runs through the property. Stella and Otis fall in stride, both going at an easy, slow trot. The rhythmic steps, warm sun, and gentle breeze course through my body and carry away my troubles.

I forgot what it feels like to be out in the open, connecting with such a majestic creature while nature carries on around me unaffected by the world and its sorrows. There's a certain perspective you can only gain from feeling small and yet tied to the outdoors and everything it contains. Breathing the same air as the birds and the bugs, soaking up the same sun as the vegetation, realizing at the end of the day we're all sustained by the same basic elements.

I didn't realize we had stopped moving and my eyes were closed until I open them again and see Noah staring right at me with a strange look on his face. Concern? Appreciation? Some intense combination of the two?

"Sorry," I whisper.

"For what, sweetheart?" He whispers back like he doesn't want to break whatever fragile peace I just found.

"Um, I don't know," I admit. "It's just a reflex."

Noah frowns, and I regret saying anything at all. I don't want his pity or the prying questions I know he wants to ask. He seems to read my thoughts and keeps his mouth shut, urging his horse to start trotting again.

We reach the stream and dismount, tying the horses to a nearby tree. I make my way to the water and Noah follows a few steps behind. I see more fence posts that need to be replaced and trees that need to be trimmed before a storm tears off a limb and throws it into the fence, damaging it further.

Noah follows my gaze and winces a bit. "Mending the fences is something we're working on. Seems like a never-ending project," he laughs dryly.

I just nod. "What else needs to be done?" I ask, trying to control my voice. All that inner peace I felt while riding Stella is slowly fading away. The to-do list takes over again, growing longer by the second. Scratch what I said last night about everything in the ranch being sturdy.

Noah stares off into the distance and adjusts his Stetson before rubbing the back of his neck with a large, calloused hand. The same hand that covered my knee last night. My skin tingles where he made contact, remembering his touch as if it branded me.

He looks like he's debating something, but in the end, he must decide to shoot straight with me. It's like his mind finally made the switch from viewing me as the boss' daughter who doesn't need to know the details to the boss who is woefully uninformed and unprepared.

"Aside from the fifty or so fence posts that need replacing, one of the irrigation tanks has a crack in it, the cattle feeder needs some serious repairs, the roof on the central barn is rotting out, the staff cabins are..."

He stops mid-sentence and wraps an arm around me, the muscles tensing and flexing as he pulls me into his side. I didn't even realize I was shaking until he squeezed me into his chest. I don't know what it is about this man and his touch, but just like at the funeral, being pressed up against Noah's solid frame calms me down.

"It's ok, darlin'. We'll get around to all of it, just give it time," he whispers into the top of my head before placing a sweet kiss there.

I know it's just a comforting gesture like a father would do for his daughter. Well, a father who wasn't mine. Yes, that has to be what it is. Noah thinks I need a new father-figure since my dad passed away. Too bad my growing feelings towards him are anything but daughterly.

"We don't have time," I whisper, softly enough I hope he didn't hear me.

Noah has to peel me off I'm clinging so hard to him, my anchor in this uncharted, scary storm.

"What's that?" He asks.

I sigh and take a step back, wrapping my arms around my torso to try and keep myself together. Almost quite literally. I feel like I might fall apart right here in front of him, crumble to the ground and blow away in the wind. Part of me thinks that might not be the worst thing. I let that thought go. No use traveling down that dark, depressing path. Not when there's so much to do.

"I spent the morning going over the finances. Rivera Ranch isn't doing so great." Saying it out loud makes the reality of the situation so much more concrete. "I have no idea what I'm doing here, what the game plan is. And on top of all that, my life in Denver won't leave me alone, and I...I don't know where to even start to fix it all."

Noah pulls me back into his chest and rests his chin on top of my head. Try as I might, I can't get rid of the feeling that we fit. He doesn't offer any solutions, nor does he try to jump in and take control in an overbearing way. He doesn't ask a million questions about Denver or why the ranch is in trouble. Instead, he holds me close, silently sharing the burden.

"It'll all be okay," he says eventually, breaking the silence. His voice rumbles through me, making me feel safe and also burning me up from the inside out. My nerves pop and my skin sizzles everywhere we're connected.

When Noah pulls away from me, I instantly feel cold and vulnerable.

Shit, get it together, girl! You cannot afford to depend on someone when your life is up in flames. You are your own constant.

Dear old Daddy taught me that one, whether he meant to or not.

"It'll be dinner time soon, and I'm the cook for the time being."

"Oh, right. Another thing we can't afford," I mumble as I turn to walk back towards the horses.

Noah wraps his hand around mine, effectively stopping me in my tracks. "Hey, now. I said everything will be okay, and I'm a man of my word. We'll get through this, Jade. That's my promise to you."

Despite overwhelming evidence to the contrary, I believe him.

Chapter 4

Noah

I was restless all night long after my ride with Jade. Flashes of her serene face tilted towards the sun plagued my mind. She was absolutely otherworldly for those few moments of peace she found. Jade was so completely mesmerizing, in fact, that my heart clenched up tight in my chest and my cock jumped to attention. Never has a woman had this effect on me.

I replayed the whole scene in my head dozens of times as I laid down for bed. The sun spilling over her lightly freckled cheeks, her creamy, slender neck exposed as she lifted her head to soak up the light and warmth, and the piercing green of her eyes when she finally opened them.

But then my thoughts turned towards the way she apologized, how she said it was instinct and brushed it off. Instead of seeing her calm, peaceful, relaxed face, I remembered how she started shivering and shaking when I listed off all the things that the ranch needed. She was no less beautiful, even when she looked up at me and confessed that the ranch was in trouble.

In fact, her vulnerability only made her more beautiful in my eyes. The way she clung to me and pressed her soft, feminine curves into my hard body had me burning up and fighting the urge to lay her out on the grass and sink eleven inches deep inside that sweet heaven between her legs. Yeah, I'm big all over and I have no doubt it'd feel amazing to stretch out her tight little pussy.

Goddamn, I've been laying here in bed for over an hour waiting for my alarm to go off, and now I have a fucking erection that I'm sure won't go away any time soon. I already jacked off twice last night to images of Jade's innocent eyes and wicked body. *Fuck*.

The more I sit with my feelings (and yes, my filthy fantasies), the more I realize I need Jade in my life. Need her like I need my next breath. The confusion and doubts fade away whenever she's around. All the questions about how and why cease to exist because the answer is always just...her.

I felt it deep in my bones the first time she fell into my arms, but my brain is finally catching up. I'll have to go slow, though. She's still working through her loss and apparently a bunch of other shit back in Denver. She might not know it yet, but she's never going back there. From what little she said in her outburst yesterday, I get the sense there's not much to go back to anyway.

I'm not going to control her or kidnap her or manipulate her into staying. I could feel the moment she surrendered to nature, the same way I do when I'm out for a ride. That's something she can't get working nine to five at a fancy job in the city, and she knows it. It'll be my job to give her more of those moments so she can be at peace in her mind, body, and soul. She belongs here. She belongs with me.

My dick finally decided to calm the fuck down enough for me to get dressed and not scare Jade away when I see her. The last thing I want is for her to think I'm some asshole only after her body. Make no mistake; I absolutely want to touch and lick and bite every inch of her and mark the creamy, delicate skin on her neck so every man knows she's mine and mine alone.

Well, shit. I'm at half-mast again thinking those dirty thoughts.

I adjust myself and head outside towards the main house to get breakfast ready. By the time I walk inside, I'm under control again.

That is until I see the object of my obsession swinging her hips to a song playing on the radio, wearing nothing but leggings and a baggy t-shirt. It's not overtly sexy, but this is Jade we're talking about. She could wear a burlap sack and still make me hard.

"Mornin' sweetheart," I say, alerting her to my presence.

She jumps in surprise and the plate she was holding shatters on the ground by her feet.

"Shit," she exclaims.

I gotta stop startling her. I wonder why she's so easily shaken up?

Jade bends down to pick up the broken pieces of the plate, but I get to her just in time. I don't even think about it, I just grab her hips and lift her up, depositing her on the counter next to the sink.

She gasps and steadies herself by clutching my biceps. Fuck, that one touch practically undoes me.

"You're barefoot," I explain when she tips her head up, giving me a questioning look. "Can't have you cutting up your pretty little feet," I grin at her, hoping to ease some of her tension.

She hasn't let go of me yet, nor have her eyes shifted away from mine. Her breathing is shallow and I can feel the little puffs of air skate across my lips. Jade must realize this at the same time I do because her hands release my arms and grip the edge of the counter instead.

Her head dips down, making some of her wild, gorgeous hair fall in front of her face. I tip her chin up and tuck her soft locks behind her ear, suppressing a groan when she parts her legs for me. I can tell she's unaware of doing so, but I take it as an invitation anyway, seizing the opportunity to step in between her legs and grip her thighs.

Jade gasps softly and then bites her bottom lip while looking up at me with big doe eyes. She's so damn pure. A little nervous, a little turned on, and a little lost. Jade moves her hands from the counter to my chest, rubbing up and down my pecs and making me go crazy with the need to feel her skin on mine.

I lean down and press my lips to her forehead. Who knew I was capable of such a tender thing? Despite the growing need to fuck her hard and fast and mark her with my teeth and cum like a goddamn animal, I also know this woman is precious and needs this from me right now.

I rub my nose up and down hers, loving the way she leans into me and flutters her eyelashes involuntarily. My lips brush against hers in the lightest of kisses. Just a hint of what's to come. She parts her little mouth so sweetly for me, letting me know she's all in.

I hover there, our lips millimeters apart, breathing the same air, both of us vibrating with desire and pent-up need. Right as I'm about to close the distance between us, the back door swings open and slams into the wall, letting us know the guys are here for breakfast.

Stepping away from Jade might have been the hardest thing I've ever had to do, but I don't want our first kiss to be witnessed by anyone. That moment will be for us and us alone to treasure. Plus, it's too soon. She already feels like my forever, but she's only been here a little over two days.

Jade gasps, then giggles when I crunch the long-forgotten broken plate under my heavy work boots. Her sweet laughter winds itself around my heart, and I know from now on I'll need it to survive.

I grin and shake my head. "Stay here while I clean this up," I tell her before heading to the closet in the corner of the kitchen where the broom is. Jade scoots across the counter until she's no longer right in front of the shattered plate, and hops down, causing me to growl at her. I didn't mean for it to come out that loud, but she could have hurt herself, dammit!

Jade raises an eyebrow at me and then smirks playfully. The little minx. Once she's officially mine, I'll spank her sweet little ass for disobeying me.

"Something smells so goooooood!" Jacob says enthusiastically as he enters the dining area. "There's no way you cooked anything that smells this incredible, Noah," Jacob teases.

"I've kept you fed for over a year now, haven't I?" I grunt. "And I don't remember you ever offering to help," I mutter as I dispose of the rest of the broken plate.

Jade bounces over to Jacob and introduces herself, shaking his hand. I get irrationally jealous of him touching any part of her, but I swallow that feeling down. I don't want to be one of those possessive assholes, but goddamn I've never felt this protective of another human being before.

"Good to meet the new boss," Jacob says, giving her that easy smile of his that I know women love. I clench and unclench my fists and remind myself that punching him in his stupid, charming face would only drive Jade away.

The tension almost leaves me completely when Jade turns back around and starts piling food onto a plate, not giving Jacob a second look. He frowns a bit, but not in a bad way. More like he's never had his smile not work on someone. I grin smugly to myself knowing I'm the only one to bring out Jade's blush and get her heart beating out of her chest.

"I've got French toast, bacon, eggs, and hashbrowns," Jade says over her shoulder, addressing Jacob and the rest of the guys who just walked in. Isaiah trails behind Cory and Zane, always the slowest of the bunch to get up in the morning.

The men perk up at that, even Isaiah, which is saying something.

"I'll take a heaping helping of everything!" Cory says enthusiastically.

"Same here," Zane adds.

"Make that four," Jacob says, speaking for both him and his twin brother, something he does often. It seems Jacob has all the words between them, but Isaiah doesn't mind. He just nods and sits at the table.

I join everyone but ignore the conversation they are having about whatever the fuck. Instead, all of my attention is focused on the way Jade moves around the kitchen. A picture of her with our kid on her hip and one growing in her belly pops into my head, making me ache for when she's my wife. I should get up and help her, but I feel like a semi-truck just slammed into my chest. The desire, the need for her is just that powerful.

Damn, if this is what love feels like, I'm certain I've never had this with anyone else. I thought I loved my ex before I found out she was cheating on me, but it's nothing, absolutely *nothing* compared to the intensity I feel towards Jade. She's broken me open and she's the only one who can put me back together. Only she'll get my heart and my fucking soul in the process and I'll get hers.

"Noah? Are you okay?" Jade asks, her face painted with concern. All of the guys are looking at me too, but they dart their eyes away when I glare at them. The fuckers snicker and exchange knowing looks. Not that it matters. Soon enough the whole world will know Jade and I are together.

"Yeah," I say after clearing my throat.

"So...breakfast?" She grins at me, probably realizing she was the cause of my lapse in brain function. It's hard to think of anything else when she's in my line of vision. Maybe I'll get used to it the longer we're together, but I get the feeling it will always be like this. She'll always be the most welcomed, sexiest, sweetest distraction. I find I wouldn't want it any other way, even if it makes me look like a fool in front of the guys.

"Breakfast sounds wonderful, darlin'," I respond, ignoring the barely audible snicker from one of the guys.

Jade smiles at me and starts to load up a plate, but I finally break free of the spell she had over me and am able to get out of my chair so I can help her, even though she's already served everyone but herself and me.

"I've got it, sweetheart, you go sit down," I tell her once we're side by side in the kitchen.

"Oh, it's fine, I can do it," she insists.

I graze my hand over the small of her back and then lightly grasp her hip, pulling her into my side. She gasps softly but doesn't pull away from me. I turn my head and kiss her temple before whispering in her ear.

"I know you can do anything and everything, darlin', but that don't mean I can't take care of you, alright?"

Her eyes are closed like she's savoring my words, and then she nods her head slowly.

"Good girl," I murmur. She shivers as soon as the words are out of my mouth. Fuck, she's not even trying to be my dream woman, but here she is, sexy as fuck and sweet as the peaches she smells like.

We somehow make it through breakfast, and the guys even manage to have some manners and not eat like the animals they can be sometimes. Jade is polite and interested in talking with everyone about what they do around the ranch and how they like their jobs. I can tell already she's winning them over. She's got this way about her that puts people at ease. She's genuine and curious, which makes it easy to talk to her. There's no doubt that everyone at the table is already loyal to her.

I tell the guys to head out while I hang back and help Jade clean up.

"You don't have to do this," she tells me, even as we stand side by side, her washing dishes while I dry them.

"What if I want to?"

"You want to do dishes?" She asks doubtfully.

"I want to spend time with you."

Her eyes widen at my response, but then that pretty pink blush returns to her cheeks as she tries to hide her smile.

"Well, in that case, would you mind if I tag along with you for the day? I want to see how everything works, what you do, get reacquainted with the ranch."

If someone were to ask to follow me around a week ago, I would have told them I don't have time to babysit. But now I want nothing more than for Jade to be attached to my hip every damn second of the day.

"Of course," I smile at her, happy beyond measure that she returns it with one of her own.

"Good. I'll go get dressed and meet you out in the stables in twenty minutes?"

"Sure thing, sweetheart," I say before dropping a kiss on top of her head like it's the most natural thing in the world.

Jade flits away, practically bouncing up the stairs with an excited energy. The thought of her peeling off her clothes and searching for the right outfit has me groaning in the best kind of agony.

I know I'm going to be fighting an obscene erection all fuckin' day, but it'll be worth it.

Chapter 5

Jade

I'm bubbling with excitement and nerves and some other feeling between my legs that makes me feel tingly and on edge. I've never felt it before, that's for sure. Only when I'm around Noah. And thinking about Noah. And being touched by Noah...

I stumble down the last stair as I make my way outside. Just thinking about the way he picked me up like I weighed nothing at all has my knees all wobbly and my feet tripping all over themselves. And let's not get started on the rush of liquid heat that pooled in my core when Noah grabbed my thighs, or how soft yet firm his lips were when he pressed them against my forehead. There was nothing fatherly about the way he was lookin' at me when he wedged his hips between my parted legs.

Nope, I can't think about those things otherwise I'll fall too far down the rabbit hole and forget why I'm here. To find money to fix the ranch and sell it. That's the goal. That's what I want. Isn't it? Yes. No. Yes.

Fuck.

I take a steadying breath and walk the rest of the way towards the stables, repeating my new mantra in my head: *Fix the ranch. Sell the ranch. Don't fall in love with Noah.*

I've almost convinced myself that I have control again when Noah turns around and smiles at me from where he's standing outside of one of the stalls. His eyes radiate warmth and safety and a sense of belonging.

I don't have the time or the space to work through all of the thoughts and feelings fighting for my attention. Not right now, at least. As much as I want to beg Noah to kiss me and fuck me and let me dissolve into him, I need to focus on the ranch.

The ranch that I may or may not want to sell. The ranch that is failing and won't get any offers anyway. The ranch where my dad lived and died. The ranch that never felt like home until right this very second.

My heart beats to the rhythm of that one word.

Home. Home. Home.

It becomes my new mantra. It courses through my veins and explodes inside of my chest. This could either be the best thing to ever happen to me or the worst. And that's saying something, considering the last week of my life.

"Jade? Are you okay?"

I snap my eyes open, not even realizing I had closed them. Noah is standing right in front of me, close enough for me to take in his cypress and rain scent, mixed with sweat and man. The combination alone has me light-headed, but when the rippling muscles of his chest and arms flex, I'm nearly brought to my knees.

"I'm good!" I squeak, needing him to back off before I spontaneously combust or keel over from a heart attack. Both of which feel like a very real possibility.

Noah smirks at me like he just figured out what my problem is. I don't even know what my problem is, so if he could diagnose me and then give me the remedy, that'd be great.

He must sense that it's all too much, and backs off. I feel both relieved and lost without his closeness.

"I lucked out when you asked if you could tag along today," he says, taking another few steps back to give me more space. I love and loathe each inch between us. What the hell is happening to me?

"Oh?" I say on an unsteady breath.

Noah just nods and grins at me. "Zane is doing a supply run in town today, which means I pick up his daily tasks."

"And what would Zane be doing if he were here?"

"Mucking the stalls."

I can tell Noah thinks I'm going to turn tail and run back inside the house, but he's wrong about that. Knowing this gives me some of my confidence back.

"I, for one, find shoveling shit to be very therapeutic," I say as I walk past him and grab one of the shovels leaning up against the back wall. The deep sound of Noah's chuckle wraps itself around my spine, making it tingle deliciously. Dangerously.

Without giving him another glance, I march over to the first stall, put on a pair of work gloves, and get to work scooping up poop and dropping it into the wheelbarrow in the corner. Silence stretches between us, but I keep focused on the task at hand. It's not the first time I've mucked the stables, though, admittedly, it's been quite a while.

I start to think I've pissed him off somehow, though I don't know what I said or did. Then again, I never knew what was going to set my dad off, either. Just when I thought I had figured out how to make him happy, he'd change his mind.

Well, fuck that. I don't have to deal with that anymore, and certainly not from someone who works on the ranch that *I* technically own. I look up towards Noah, expecting to see him fuming or pouting, but instead, he's staring right at me with a look I can't place.

"What?" I snap, defensively.

"How the hell can you be so beautiful even when you're ankle-deep in horse shit?"

The ridiculousness of his statement, the shock of him being captivated instead of angry, and the whiplash of memories from my childhood...all of it roars through me and comes out as laughter.

I let the sensation take over until I'm gasping for air. God, it feels good to laugh. I feel lighter than I have in years. I can feel some of the heaviness roll off my shoulders as they shake with more laughter.

When I finally have myself under control, I let my eyes wander back to where Noah is standing. He looks amused, if not a little surprised at my reaction.

"While that wasn't a joke, I'm sure glad to hear your laughter, darlin'," he drawls, tipping his lips up in a sexy little grin.

I feel the blush creeping up into my cheeks, but I manage to roll my eyes at him in an attempt to cover up how his every word seems to burn through me.

"You don't have to keep mucking the stalls," he says after a few moments of silence between us.

"I said I wanted to tag along and get reacquainted with the ranch. I can't very well do that if I just sit on the sidelines and watch, now can I?"

"I wouldn't mind you watchin' me," he says under his breath. I'm not sure if he meant for me to hear him or not, but the comment makes my pussy clench. Which, I know, is ridiculous, but there it is.

Ignoring him and the way he makes me feel, I return to the task at hand. With the two of us working, it only takes about an hour to clean the stalls. Next, we brush and feed the five horses we have. Noah catches me up on the new ones we've acquired since I've been gone, as well as the ones we either sold or had to put down.

Seeing the way his eyes light up when he's taking care of the horses makes my heart melt a little for him. He's gentle and steady when he's handling them. Kind of like he is with me. I remember Noah from before I left. He was gruff, though not unkind towards most people, but he's always been sweet to me. It's not helping my confusing emotions.

I can't seem to take my eyes off his large hands and how they gently pet the horse's neck, nose, or flank. It makes me wonder what his hands would feel like petting me. Roaming over my shoulders, my chest, lower...

Stella shakes her silky mane out, drawing my attention back to her and away from my dirty thoughts. My eyes dart over to Noah, but he's busy getting a treat for Otis and Charlie.

I smile softly to myself when I think of Charlie. My dad thought it was the most clever and hilarious name. Charlie horse. Get it? Cue the eye roll at the lame dad joke. Charlie was one of the first horses I remember as a little girl growing up on the ranch. He was born right here and has been with us ever since. I was afraid he might have died in the time I was away, but I'm glad the old man is still here. Who would have thought that horse would outlive my dad?

"Do you need a break, or are you ready for our next task?" Noah asks, breaking me out of the surprisingly sweet memory. It's confusing to remember the good parts of growing up here. They've been overshadowed by my anger for so long.

"What do you think?" I respond with an eyebrow raised in challenge.

"I think you should take a break, but I also think you're not gonna do a damn thing I say," he says with a bit of a scowl.

"You're a quick learner," I grin.

Before I know it, Noah and I have been at it for hours. We stopped briefly for lunch and then to check in on Jacob, Isaiah, and Cory, who are working on herding the red Angus cattle to a new pasture. Now we're back out by the creek, working on replacing the fence posts I noticed yesterday.

Every muscle in my body screams in protest as I carry the old, rotted fence post to the trailer hitched to the back of one of the quads. I'm sticky from a mixture of sweat and dirt, my hair is a frizzy mess, and I can feel the blisters on my feet from wearing my old boots that never quite fit right. I'm achy down to my very bones.

I've never felt better.

Yes, I'm gross, but I'm also free. A light breeze kisses my cheeks and whips through my hair, providing a refreshing break from the heat. I inhale deeply, letting the scent of grass, mud, and wood, with a hint of cypress from Noah fill my lungs.

I didn't know how much I missed this. I never allowed myself to miss anything about the ranch. It was easier that way. Seeing things in black and white helped me justify leaving the way I did, without so much as a goodbye to the town. My dad knew, of course, and he didn't try to stop me.

I'm suddenly hit with the memory of that day. It's one I pushed out of my mind years ago. I had been planning my escape for months. Sent my resume to anywhere and everywhere I thought might hire a soon-to-be high school graduate with little to no real-world experience. The only factor in my job search was that it had to be out of state.

I just had to wait until I graduated high school, and then I could leave it all behind. I wasn't sure when to break the news to my dad. I was eighteen by the time I graduated, and with my final obligation out of the way, freedom was within reach.

My dad stood proudly at the graduation ceremony and hugged me tight when it was all over. We went to the most popular restaurant in town and ordered appetizers, dinner, and dessert. He even let me have a sip of his whiskey. Dad went on and on about how proud of me he was, how I had a bright future ahead of me, how this milestone was just one of many great things I was going to accomplish.

I truly believe he meant the words when said them. He always did. Which made it all the harder to reconcile the other side of him. I learned to hold on to his praise loosely, as he had a way of turning on a dime and throwing the words right back at me.

Sure enough, by the time we got home, something had changed. I knew it before we even got out of the truck. Like always, I had no idea what I did wrong, but I could pinpoint the moment he switched from a loving, kind father to an unstable, intimidating asshole.

It was in the silence.

We were talking about the ranch and I was saying something, I don't even remember what, but he just stopped responding to me. I tried starting up the conversation again, but he tightened his grip on the steering wheel and took measured breaths like he was barely holding back the demons inside of him.

The silence was heavy and all-consuming, threatening to shatter around me and cut me deep like it had done so many times before.

We were barely in the front door when he screamed at me for not taking my shoes off as soon as I got inside. Of course, I slipped them off a second after he told me to, trying to get things back on the right track. That wasn't good enough either, though.

Don't just leave them on the floor! I'm always cleaning up your goddamn messes. You're an adult now, if you can't even put your shoes away, how do you expect to survive in the real world? How? Tell me, Jade. Don't you dare cry on me, your tears mean fuck all.

He grabbed the heels I bought specially for graduation, and threw them into the wall behind me, a foot or so away from my head. That's when I knew. Now or never.

I told him right then and there I was leaving for Denver in the morning, even though I hadn't planned on going for another few weeks. I figured it would be easy enough to change my bus ticket.

Dad froze in place. I saw a kaleidoscope of emotions flicker in his eyes, clear green like mine. Anger, disbelief, sadness, disgust, but above all, loneliness. That look is seared into my brain, I just chose to ignore it these last few years. He didn't say anything to me, he just turned around and went upstairs to his room, slamming the door.

That was the last time I saw him. We talked over the years, in fact, I called him a few weeks after I got settled in. He acted like nothing happened, as per usual. And that was that.

I hear an echo, some far off sound tugging at my brain, but I can't quite hang on to it long enough.

I feel like I'm being split in two, both good and bad memories of growing up here contradict each other and race through my brain as if they are competing. Fresh air and suffocation. Laughter and heartbreak. Abandonment and belonging. Hot and cold, up and down, praise and condemnation. I'm teetering on the edge.

That sound filters through my consciousness again, louder this time.

"Jade? Jade? What's wrong?"

The deep rumble stills my thoughts.

"Talk to me, baby, are you okay?"

I nod my head, the world around me slowly coming back into focus. "Sorry," I whisper, hating how weak I sound.

"Nothing to be sorry for, sweetheart," he says softly, standing right in front of me. "Tell me what you were just thinking about that made you so upset."

"Just workin' through some stuff is all," I say, more confidently this time.

"What the hell were you working through that had you turning white as a sheet and damn near passing out?"

I shake my head back and forth, unwilling to go back to that place to try and explain it all to him. "It doesn't matter. It's all in the past."

Noah reaches out and cups my jaw, tilting my head up so I have to meet his gaze. "Darlin', if it's still affecting you like that, it ain't in your past."

I jerk my head out of his hand and step back, wrapping my arms around myself. "Whether it's my past or present isn't your concern," I spit out, needing him to stop trying to untangle the knot of unresolved guilt deep in my gut. "It's *mine*. *My* past, *my* memories, *my* decision on what to do with the ranch."

He takes a step forward, but I take one back. I retreat as he advances, all the way until my back hits the huge oak tree at the edge of the property.

Noah cages me in with a hand on either side of my head. I look up at his fierce, but always kind eyes, and stick my chin out in defiance.

"What you don't understand yet, baby girl, is that *you* are *mine*."

Before I can even process everything his statement implies, Noah crashes his lips down on mine, pushing his tongue inside my mouth and possessing me completely. His kiss is wild and fierce like he's trying to override all of the other thoughts in my head and replace them with him and only him.

His tongue slides against mine as he explores my depths, each stroke of his tongue seems to incite a deeper frenzy within him, one that matches mine. All of me is consumed by all of him. His smell, his taste, the heat radiating off of his chiseled body.

I moan when I feel his fingers tangle in my messy hair and tug, angling me just right so he can slide in deeper. His Stetson falls off, but he doesn't notice. It's like he can't get enough of me. I already know I'll never get enough of him.

Noah presses me into the tree with his body, allowing me to feel his need for this. For me. It's intoxicating.

He's hot and hard where I'm wet and aching for him. He tears his mouth from mine to kiss my neck and the curve of my shoulder, alternating between open-mouthed kisses and sharp little nips. My entire body tingles with anticipation, my skin humming. His hands roam up and down my curves, his words and fingers worshiping them.

Noah makes his way back up to my mouth, sipping at my lips this time, dipping his tongue inside and teasing me before retreating and starting over again. When I fist his shirt where it clings to his ribs and pull him closer, Noah growls and deepens the kiss, grabbing my ass and rubbing me up and down his hard length.

One minute we're fused together, and the next minute he's gone.

I open my eyes only to see him pick up his hat and back away from me. "I'm sorry," he grunts before jumping on his quad and driving off.

I'm too stunned to do anything but lean against the tree and brush my fingers over my swollen lips.

Chapter 6

Noah

Jade has been at the ranch for a week now, and I don't know how much longer I can hold back. I can't believe I practically mauled the girl her third day here, and right when she was in the middle of a breakdown, no less.

She had been quiet and thoughtful throughout that day she was following me around. Jade worked hard, and damn if that wasn't just as much of a turn on as her bright green eyes and curvy little body.

I stopped to appreciate the lean muscles in her arms while she was carrying an old fence post, and had to bite back a moan when the breeze combed through her hair and wafted her sweet peaches and cream scent in my direction. Even after a day of hard labor on the ranch, Jade managed to smell amazing.

But then something changed. Her brows knit together, her breathing hitched, and she looked like she was about to collapse. I tried calling out to her, but she was stuck in some awful place.

Jade, stubborn as ever, hardly gave me any information other than she was working through some shit. It doesn't take a genius to figure out she means her dad. I don't know what happened between them, but it's clear their relationship wasn't the picture-perfect little family her father always portrayed to the public.

She was fierce and fragile and determined to keep me at arms' length. Yeah, fuck that. I couldn't stand the thought of her pushing me away without knowing the depths of my devotion to her. So, I did the only thing my stupid, lust-filled brain could think of.

I kissed the ever-living fuck out of her.

And damn if she didn't kiss me right back. One taste of those honey lips and I was lost. Completely gone for her. I kissed her like I needed the air in her lungs to breathe, and in that moment, I'm pretty sure I did. Still do.

But I had to back off. I was ready to rip her clothes off and fuck away whatever sadness and pain she's wrestling with. The kicker is, I'm pretty sure she was right there with me. The way she rolled her soft body against my hard one, her little gasps and moans of pleasure, the way she surrendered to my touch...

Fuck. It's all I've been able to think about since I pried my body away from hers.

It had to be done, however. Jade was in no state of mind to be making decisions like that, and I all but took her choice away. I hate that I took advantage of her. All I wanted was to comfort her, make her see that she's not alone, that I'm always going to be here to share in her sorrow as well as her joy.

We've been cordial since that day. Polite. Professional. I fucking loathe it. But if she needs space, then I can give that to her. For now. Even if it's killing me.

As I make my way towards the main house to prepare breakfast, I see that Jade has beaten me to it. Again. I swear the woman doesn't know how to take a break. Which is saying something coming from me. I can't remember the last time I left the ranch other than for a supply run. But at least I shut my brain off at night when I get in from supper. Jade, on the other hand, cleans up after us, despite our protests, and then locks herself away in the office for hours on end. I can see the light shining through the corner window from my cabin and I know she can't be getting more than a handful of hours of sleep every night.

Opening the back door that leads into the kitchen, I take a moment to appreciate Jade before she notices me. Even from where I'm standing, I can tell she's bone-tired. Beautiful, but wrecked. She's not bouncing on her feet like she sometimes does when she's barefoot in the kitchen. Yes, despite my hounding her to wear shoes at all times since the morning she broke the plate, the bull-headed woman trots around with her cute little feet unprotected. It makes me want to spank her and also kiss each and every painted toe on her perfect feet.

I notice her sighing every thirty seconds or so like she has to remember to take full breaths. She leans on the counter while waiting for the coffee to brew instead of tending to the rest of breakfast like she's done every other morning. Jade is an excellent multi-tasker, which is just one more thing that makes her an excellent ranch owner. I know she doesn't see it that way, but after years of working on many different ranches, I know a good boss when I meet one.

This morning, however, she can't seem to muster up the energy to do more than one thing at a time. I feel helpless. I've told her to take a break, I've tried sending her away from the stables, from mending fences, and even from trying to trim a tree all by her damn self. It's a wonder the girl hasn't gotten seriously hurt. But every single time I tell her to go back to the house and grab some water and a nap, I find her somewhere else doing another big project she shouldn't be doing by herself.

There's no doubt about it, Jade is determined to fix up this place. Whether it's to sell or to keep is anyone's guess. I'm hoping she wants to stay, but I haven't gotten up the courage to ask her yet. Every once in a while, I'll catch her smiling to herself when she's taking care of one of the horses or on the porch swing, sipping a glass of sweet tea. I'd like to think that means she likes it here and she's slowly moving past whatever trauma took place here during her childhood.

Jade turns around to grab a mug and spots me just standing in the doorway, watching her like the obsessed, lovesick puppy I've become. The one she's made me without even trying.

"Mornin'," I tip my hat to her while making my way to the kitchen.

"Hey, Noah," she answers, her voice groggy with sleep. I notice dark circles under her beautiful eyes. Even the green of her irises is faded.

"You okay, darlin'?"

She whips her head up to meet my gaze. I haven't used any endearments with her since our kiss, but seeing her this worn-out has me ready to scoop her up and tie her to the bed so she'll get some sleep. I can think of some other things she might enjoy while tied to her bed...

"I'm fine," she says, pulling me out of my dirty thoughts. "Just couldn't sleep last night on account of the big meetin' and all this afternoon."

It's the most information Jade has given me in days. Our conversations mostly consist of her asking what needs to be done, me telling her the guys and I have it under control, and then her ignoring me until I try to get her to go back into the house. It's not that I think she's incapable of working the ranch, not at all. It's just that she's going to run herself ragged, burning both ends of the candle like this. At any rate, she hasn't told me about a meeting, so I try to gently pry more information out of her.

"With the lawyer?" I ask, feigning like we've talked about it before.

"The agent from the life insurance company. He's had me doing all this digging into Dad's medical history, his work on the ranch, even his marriage with my momma. I tried answering to the best of my ability, but I feel so awful not knowing a lot of the more recent stuff since I haven't been here."

I take a few steps into the kitchen, needing to be closer to her. I don't know if it's the exhaustion that has her opening up to me, or the clear anxiety she has over the meeting today, but I want to savor every word she's giving me.

"You had your reasons," I say softly, hoping to ease some of her guilt. "Besides, what's done is done. All we can do is move forward, alright, sweetheart?"

I think she might shut down at another endearment, but instead, she gazes up at me with unshed tears in her eyes. Damn, this woman and her tears. They gut me every time. Just as quickly as they appear, however, Jade blinks them away and turns to pour some coffee in the mug she got out for herself. She hands it over to me, that Southern hospitality shining through once again.

I know better than to refuse Jade anything, so I take the mug and give her my thanks.

Cory and Zane stumble inside, followed by Jacob, and finally Isaiah. I guess our little chat is over. Hopefully, I can convince Jade to stay inside and get ready for her meeting instead of helping out on the ranch this morning. One more look in her direction tells me I won't have to work very hard. The woman is barely functioning as it is, and she won't be able to put up much of a fight.

I know the guys notice the change in Jade's demeanor, and they make a point to have a quiet conversation and thank her for the food, as well as clean up after themselves. She doesn't even protest as she downs her third cup of coffee.

***

I haven't seen Jade since breakfast. She wasn't around the ranch, which had me hoping she was finally taking some time to relax. However, considering the state of mind she was in this morning, I doubt she was able to do anything but worry about the future.

Lunch around here is a free for all. We can go to the main house and warm up leftovers or make sandwiches. It's all well and good, except it means I didn't have an excuse to see Jade in the middle of the day.

Now it's just past three in the afternoon, and I'm worried. Maybe I shouldn't be. Some part of me hoped she'd come tell me how the meeting went, but I have to remind myself that she's not in love with me yet. Not the way I am with her. But she'll get there, I'm sure of it.

The universe must be listening in to my thoughts because I see Jade walk out of the house and head towards the stables. No, she's not walking, she's running. Something about that has my entire body tense and on high alert. I run to the stables as well, but I'm farther away than she is.

I get there just in time to see her storm off on Stella.

"Jade!" I yell after her, to no avail. "Goddamnit, woman," I grunt as I saddle up Bolt, our fastest horse. She's going to kill herself riding like that. She was completely out of control. Even in the brief glimpse of her I got, I could feel the fear and fury radiating off of her tiny body.

By the time I have Bolt ready to go, I've lost sight of Jade and Stella, but I have a pretty good idea of where they might end up. Bolt and I pick up speed as I push him to his limit. Flashes of Jade being thrown from Stella plague my mind and have me urging the powerful beast even faster.

When I get to the stream running through the east side of the property, I see Stella tied around a tree and Jade hurling rocks into the water, sobbing. I know whatever I'm about to walk into will be a gut-wrenching and defining moment for us, but at least she's not physically hurt.

I dismount and tie Bolt up next to Stella, giving him a gentle pat on his neck to show my appreciation for his efforts to get us here so fast.

Slowly, as if approaching a wild, scared horse, I make my way to the edge of the stream where Jade is. I'm not sure how to alert her to my presence without startling her like I've done so many times before, so I just observe her for a moment. Her face is red and blotchy, both from tears and anger. She bends down and grabs a big rock and chucks it into the moving water with a grunt. It splashes water on her, but that only seems to fuel her anger.

Jade yells and kicks the water as if it splashed her on purpose. Then, she picks up another large rock and throws it forcefully downstream. Only this time, she cries out and clutches her hand. That's all I need to see before closing the distance between us.

"Let me see your hand," I demand, more forcefully than I meant to. I can't help it; this woman has me completely frayed at the edges with worry.

"Don't you fuckin' touch me, Noah," she yells, stepping away from me.

"I just want to see if you're hurt," I try again, softer this time.

"I'm fine, see? Just a scrape." She flashes her hand at me so I can see the scrape on her palm. It's not deep, but I still hate the idea of her being hurt.

"Let me take you back home and get a bandage on that," I offer in a calm voice, hoping to de-escalate the situation.

"Home? *Home*?!" She laughs bitterly. "I don't have a home, Noah. And neither will you soon enough." She's silent for a few seconds and then a fresh round of tears covers her cheeks. She tries wiping them away, but more spill out until she gives up the fight and just lets them fall.

"Talk to me, Jade. What's going on? The meeting with the insurance agent didn't go well?"

"Yeah, I guess you could say that. They ruled my dad's death a suicide, which means they won't payout."

I'm stunned. Could it be true? Is there something we could have done to help him? What does this mean for Jade? I take a step closer to the stubborn, beautiful, broken woman who has my heart.

"I mean, what the fuck?!" she screams, staring off into the stream, no doubt thinking about punishing the water with another rock. Jade takes a breath and continues on, quieter this time. "Dad was a lot of things, but not suicidal. Right? And now what? They closed the case so that's that. The asshole said I could fight it, but I don't have the resources for that. No insurance money. No ranch. No place to go and no money to go there anyway. What the fuck am I supposed to do, Noah? I didn't want any of this, I didn't want to come back, but now I don't think I want to leave..."

Jade drags in a shaky breath and starts sobbing, only she's all cried out, so it just comes out as these heartbreaking gasps for air. I close the distance between us and catch her right before she collapses onto the ground.

"No!" she screams in my face, pushing against me with everything she has left. I know she's not really fighting me, she's fighting against the uncertainty, the unfairness, the fear. I hold her tighter as she works out her aggression. "Let me go, you asshole!"

"Not a chance," I murmur softly while pinning her arms down so she can't claw at my chest anymore. Not that she's hurting me, but I'm afraid she's going to aggravate the cuts on her hand.

"Stop, you have to stop," she begs. There's anger in her voice but also defeat. "Stop showing up here, stop holding me when I'm falling apart, stop making me think you want me, and then running away."

"Jade, sweetheart..." Her words pain me, especially when I realize I contributed to her current state of mind. Does she really think I don't want her? We have to discuss that later, right now I need her to start breathing before she passes out.

"Enough," she yells again, her energy and aggression spiking before the inevitable crash. "I don't need saving. I get it, I'm a pathetic, lonely little girl who doesn't know what she's doing. I hate that you're always seeing me at my absolute worst points."

With that, Jade gives up the fight and leans into me, allowing my strength to hold her up. I cup the back of her head and tuck it into my chest, while my other hand keeps a steady hold of her around her waist.

"If this is you at your worst, then I'm thankful I could be here. And I can't wait to be here for your best," I say into the shell of her ear.

"You... You can't possibly mean that," she whispers, hiccupping at the end.

I massage the back of her neck and bury my nose in her untamed, red hair, letting her peaches and cream scent wash over me. How do I respond to her doubts? She has no idea the lengths I would go to for her, but I don't want to scare her off with declarations of love and promises of forever.

"A wise woman once told me I should be stubborn about the right things," I murmur softly as I tip her head up so I can look into those gorgeous green eyes of hers. Even puffy and rimmed in red, they are beautiful in a way that almost hurts. "And you, Jade, are the right thing to be stubborn about. I refuse to let you think you're all alone in the world. I refuse to let you deal with all of this on your own. I refuse to let you go."

I rest my forehead on hers and encourage her to match my breathing. When her pulse slows down and her breathing somewhat returns to normal, I guide her over to the horses. She starts to untie Stella, but I stop her by gently grabbing her wrist and tugging her to the side. Jade doesn't fight me this time. Good girl. She's learning to trust me, and fuck, that thought makes my chest swell up with pride.

When I've tied Stella up to Bolt, I help Jade up on Bolt's saddle before climbing on behind her and heading back towards the stables at a slow, steady pace. I can tell Jade is completely worn out, which is why I didn't want her riding by herself.

I feel her little body melt against me. She rests her head on my shoulder and I wrap my arm around her waist, pulling her close and holding her in place.

"I'm sorry," she whispers into the side of my neck where her face is buried. I almost don't hear it.

"There's nothing to be sorry for, sweetheart. You gotta stop apologizing when nothing is your fault, okay?" She nods, but I know this won't be the last time we have this conversation.

I hold my beautiful Jade in my arms and absorb her pain. She's this strong, stubborn, driven woman, who has a shy, vulnerable side as well. Whatever happened to her has left her with defenses a mile high and a fragile, timid heart underneath.

Jade lets me help her down off of Bolt and waits for me while I put the horses away. We walk in silence up to the house and I scoop her up in my arms once we get inside. She curls up into me and lets me take her to her room.

Jade looks up at me while I pull back the covers, her eyes never leaving mine as I remove her shoes and socks. She's still looking at me when I guide her to lay back on the sheets. Those green eyes of hers wander up and down my body while I take my hat and boots off and climb in bed next to her so we're facing each other, pulling the blankets over us.

I reach out and tuck some of her gorgeous red hair behind her ear, and then pull her close so I can kiss her forehead.

"Rest now, darlin'," I whisper into her soft skin.

Jade lifts her head slightly so we're eye to eye, nose to nose, our lips inches apart. I barely get the words out of my mouth before Jade presses her soft lips into mine. I can't help but kiss her back. I know somewhere in the back of my mind that this is another situation where she's emotionally and physically exhausted and I shouldn't be taking advantage of that, but fuck it, I need her. And she needs me right now. I can taste it.

Jade owns me, body and soul, and this kiss sealed her fate. Her lithe little body presses into me and I grab her hip to pull her even closer. Jade snakes her arm around my neck and holds me close while she tangles her tongue with mine. I feel the kiss growing heated and leading to more, so I pull away from her. She's not ready for that yet, but soon.

"Did I do something wrong?" she pants, her eyes round and glossed over, her brow furrowed in confusion.

"Not at all, sweetheart. Love kissing these soft lips," I whisper, giving her a brief kiss to prove my point. "But you need to rest. We'll work out everything else when you wake up. Just close your eyes, baby. Close your eyes and rest now."

Jade nods and rolls over, giving me her back. I wrap my body around her much smaller one and pull her into my chest, kissing the back of her neck before nuzzling my head into her shoulder.

I whisper soothing things into her soft skin until she goes limp in my arms.

"I love you, Jade," I say before drifting off to sleep myself.

Chapter 7

Jade

For the second time since coming back to the ranch, I wake up smelling like cypress and rain.

Noah.

I peek one eye open, half excited and half nervous for what I might find in my bed. I can't help the surge of disappointment that courses through my veins when I discover I'm alone. One look at the clock tells me I've been asleep for nearly twelve hours. It's just before four in the morning, about the time I'd normally wake up to make breakfast.

Scenes from the previous day come flooding back. The awful insurance agent, cold and calloused, telling me my father committed suicide and I won't be getting a check. As if that's all I care about. Yes, the money is important, but my dad...

I can't go there. That's why I went to the stables instead like I had done so many times before.

As a little girl, I often went down to the stream when things got intense at home. I used to picture each rock as a worry or a hurt in my heart as I tossed it into the stream. I gave my burdens to the water and returned home lighter, ready to do it all over again.

But yesterday, the worries and hurts were too big.

Until Noah showed up. He was all kind eyes, strong shoulders, and tender touches. I may have been a total wreck, but Noah was solid as ever, soaking up my tears and my fists and giving out only peace and strength. Will he still be there for me when the ranch goes under? Where do we even stand?

I grunt in frustration and throw the blankets off. I have so many uncertainties in my life right now, but I've gotta put on my big girl panties and start making some decisions one way or another. Starting with Noah.

I quickly get dressed and make my way to the kitchen, where I find Noah already working on breakfast. He looks up, those warm, calming brown eyes of his meeting mine.

"Mornin', sweetheart," he drawls, making me blush. I like all of his endearments, though I'd never tell him that. They make me feel precious, which is an entirely new thing for me.

"Hey," I say back, still not sure what he really thinks about me after everything yesterday. Before I can let my doubts get away from me, Noah strides over to where I'm standing and cups my face, holding me still while his lips melt into mine.

I moan as Noah deepens our kiss. He breathes me in, consuming me completely, controlling me with powerful strokes of his tongue. I have to break the kiss to pull more oxygen into my lungs, but Noah continues kissing and biting his way down to my shoulder, where he rests his head.

"Don't leave me," I whisper, wrapping my arms around his torso as if I could keep him with me forever.

Noah lifts his head from my shoulder so he can rub his nose up and down mine like he did that first day in the kitchen. It's such a sweet gesture, grounding, even. It feels like home. Everything about this man.

"Never, darlin'. And I wasn't leaving you before, I was just giving you space to process," he tells me, his deep timbre rolling through me, making me feel safe and totally turned on.

"I don't need space," I whisper, his lips inches from mine.

"What do you need?"

"You."

I kiss him this time, pouring out all of me, every confusing emotion, every unanswered question, every thought of home and belonging, all of my pain, and all of my hopes, however far away they seem at the moment. He swallows them down and gives all of himself to me as well.

"Whoooop! Get it, old man!" Jacob's enthusiastic yell is followed by laughter and catcalls from the other guys as they filter in for breakfast. Even Isaiah is smiling, which is rare.

I bury my head in Noah's chest, embarrassed that we were caught, but still buzzing from having his lips on mine. Noah just chuckles and kisses the top of my head. "I'm all yours, Jade. You own me," he whispers so only I can hear.

***

Since Noah cooked, I cleaned up. They guys went off to do the chores and work on whatever projects were left over from the day before, and I went up to the office to try and figure out a way out of this mess.

That was ten hours ago. Noah stopped in briefly around noon to drop a sandwich off for me, but I couldn't afford to let the tanned, muscled, Greek god of a man distract me. I want to save the ranch for me, but more than that, I want to save the ranch for him. It's clear he loves his job, and I love... Well, let's just get the ranch figured out first. I'll deal with my feelings later.

I've called my dad's lawyer and financial advisor. Both gave me free phone consultations that were ultimately unfruitful. Same goes for finding other revenue streams that don't have a huge upfront cost to renovate or hire more workers.

I just need to find some money. Adam's weaselly face pops into my head. Not that I'd ask him for money, God no. Nor would I ask for my old job back. But maybe he would consider at least giving me a recommendation letter for my next potential employer? If I can find something around here that makes decent money and work on the biggest projects with the guys on the weekends, maybe, just maybe...

In a moment of weakness, I turn my phone on for the first time in days. I regret it as soon as the missed calls and texts come through. All from Adam.

Adam: Don't be like this, it was a misunderstanding.

Adam: You better not have gone to HR. I swear you'll regret it, you bitch.

Adam: Don't act like you're innocent here. Did you really think you were promoted up to my department based on your high school diploma and work ethic?

Adam: Fuck you. You're not better than me. You'll see.

I shudder when I read his last text. I don't bother listening to the voicemails.

Just then, there's a light knock on the office door, and then Noah walks in. He smiles but then furrows his brow in concern. "Everything okay?"

"Other than the obvious?" I ask sarcastically, spreading my arms out over the messy desk full of notes and research and budgets.

I was hoping to deflect, but I can tell Noah doesn't quite buy it. He lets it go for now.

"So, what's the plan, boss?" He grins at me and winks before taking his hat off and combing his fingers through his dark hair. I'm momentarily frozen in place, just watching the beautiful man in front of me. It's really not fair that someone as built and chiseled as Noah *also* has a devastating smile and sparkling eyes. It should be illegal or something.

I clear my throat and try to piece together what he just asked me so I can respond. The ranch. The plan. Right.

"Well, our problem is that we need money. And we don't have any," I deadpan, standing up from the desk and walking towards him.

"Ah, yes, I hear that's not good for business, huh?" He grins.

"Not particularly," I sigh. "Not unless you and the other workers want to take a pay cut for the next year and use your salaries to invest back into the ranch."

Noah looks like he's considering it.

"Noah, I'm kidding. Obviously. I wouldn't actually ask any of you to do that."

"I know. But what if I could help you out?"

"No," I say forcefully, even as I find myself drifting closer and closer to him. It's like he has some gravitational pull and I'm helpless to do anything but get caught up in him.

"No? That's it? You're not even going to hear me out?"

"Does it involve you giving me money?"

"Ye—"

"Then no."

"Now, hold on a goddamn minute, if you'd just—"

"Noah, please," I cut him off. "There's no reason to make this whole thing that much more complicated. You don't even know how much I need, first of all, and second of all, say you loan me the money and I can't pay you back? Or what if you decided to leave before the investment pays off? Or what if…" I trail off, my face turning red, but needing to finish the thought. "What if whatever is happening between us ends poorly. Then I'd really be fucked."

Noah's eyes flash darkly as he closes the distance between us. His hands grip my hair and tug, forcing me to meet his gaze. "Oh, I'll fuck you, darlin'. No need to worry about that." His voice is low and gravelly, sending a shiver down my spine. He notices, grinning like the arrogant bastard he is.

But then his smoldering eyes turn soft. It pulls at something in my chest, and I find myself almost ready to spill all of my secrets to this man. "As for the rest," Noah continues, kissing my temple and ghosting his lips over the shell of my ear. "I'm not going anywhere, Jade. You're mine and I'm yours, I thought we already had that talk."

Everything in my brain is screaming that he's a lyin' sack of shit and that if I trust him, the other shoe that's always threatening to drop finally will. But my damn fool heart is ready to throw itself at the gorgeous cowboy, despite the consequences.

His hands glide down my back and grip my hips, pulling me closer to him. I flatten my palms over his chest for support, and then slowly slide them up to loop around his neck. Noah rubs his nose up and down mine, making my tummy flutter.

"Does this mean you're thinking about staying here for good?" he murmurs before placing a light kiss on the corner of my mouth. I turn towards him so I can kiss him for real, but he moves out of the way and grins at me when I pout. "Answer the question and I'll give you whatever you want," he whispers, kissing the other corner of my mouth before resting his forehead on mine.

I want to stay, but I'm afraid that if I voice that thought, the universe will take it all away from me.

"Just say yes, sweetheart. Tell me you're staying. Tell me you're mine."

Noah kisses across my jaw, down my neck, and over my collarbone. I find myself nodding, going along with his demands so I can have more of his skin on my skin. I want to give him everything, all of me. I want him to be my first, and I pray he'll be my last. My only.

"Tell me," he demands, growling into the hollow of my neck before licking me there.

"Yes," I moan.

"Yes, what?" he grunts, kissing his way back up my neck and pulling my earlobe in between his teeth.

"Yes, I'm staying. Yes, I'm yours," I breathe out.

"Damn right you are," he says right before claiming my lips as his own. All other thoughts and worries about the future fall right out of my head. All I can focus on is being backed into the desk and lifted up by Noah's hands on my thighs.

I part my legs for him and whimper when he steps in between them and rubs his hard cock over my center.

"Fuck, I feel your heat, darlin'. Are you wet for me? Do you need this?" He thrusts his hips, hitting my clit through the thin material of my yoga pants and panties.

"Yes, yes, I need you." The words just come pouring out of my mouth, almost without my permission.

Noah kisses me again and again, each swipe of his tongue wiping away my fears and doubts until all that's left is his taste, his smell, his touch.

"Please," I gasp, though I'm not even sure what I'm asking for.

Noah grunts and rubs his fingers against my pussy, over the fabric of my clothes. I grind down on his hand and bury my face in his shoulder to muffle my cries.

"Jesus, you're so damn responsive. I'm hardly even touching you," he grunts.

"So why don't you touch me for real?"

His eyes go dark and his jaw tenses right before he crashes his lips on mine and kisses the breath right out of my lungs. When he tears himself away from me, it's so he can kneel down and press his face into my core, inhaling my scent through the fabric of my clothes.

Noah growls and dips his thumbs into the waistband of my pants. I lift my hips up and watch as he peels my yoga pants and panties off in one swift move.

"This okay, Jade?" he asks, pausing with his hands on my knees, looking me in the eyes to make sure I mean what I say.

I nod. "I want to feel you. I've always wondered what it would be like..." My face burns up at my words, knowing I just gave my inexperience away.

"You've never had anyone taste this juicy cunt, baby?"

His words are so filthy and so...hot. I shake my head no.

"Have you ever had anyone inside of you, Jade?"

I close my eyes, not wanting to answer his question and admit just how innocent I really am.

"Tell me, darlin', tell me I'm the only one, fucking tell me, Jade," he demands.

"Only you," I whisper, finally opening my eyes.

"Jesus, you're perfect."

With that, he yanks my legs wide open so I'm spread out before him on the desk. Noah flattens his tongue and takes a long, slow lick up the seam of my pussy, stopping to flick my clit and suck on the swollen ball of nerves.

I moan and fall back on the desk, allowing Noah to guide one of my legs over his shoulder, and then the other. I tilt my head up and watch Noah as he stares at my pussy. Something about that is inexplicably hot. I feel myself clench up, and then more of my juices leak out of me.

"So fucking wet..." Noah growls before shoving his face in between my thighs and making me crazy with need.

He's eating me out in desperate, forceful strokes. I feel his tongue plunge inside of my tight little hole, in and out, and then back up to circle my clit. I cry out and claw the desk, seeking something to keep me grounded during this hurricane of pleasure.

Noah pulls back for a second, making me whine in frustration. He grabs my hands and puts them on his head. I instantly fist his hair, which causes him to grunt in approval.

"You need to hang on to something, you hang on to *me*, darlin.'"

I nod and shove his head in between my legs again, making him chuckle into my soaking wet folds. I feel the vibrations every-fucking-where, putting me right on the edge.

Noah sucks on my clit and thrusts a finger inside of me without warning. I moan at the unexpected invasion and then wiggle my hips to get him to go deeper.

He leans back slightly so he can watch himself fuck me with his finger. The sloppy wet sounds fill the small room and make me tremble in anticipation. I can't contain the whimper that spills out when he adds a second finger. I'm close, so, so close...

Noah's eyes snap to mine. He looks at me like he's going to rip me to shreds with his intense desire. I can't wait to let him. I slam my eyes shut as a delicious wave of ecstasy sweeps through my body and rattles my bones.

"Fuck, that's it, sweetheart, goddamn, this juicy cunt," he grunts before leaning down and sucking on my clit in time with the thrusts of his fingers.

I hold my breath as my muscles draw up tight. For a moment I'm suspended in empty space, hovering, flying. The hard, merciless rhythm of his tongue is almost painful on my clit, overwhelming in the most glorious way. He twists his fingers and curls them up, breaking the tension over my body as the first wave of my orgasm floods through me.

I bow my back off of the desk and cry out, my legs slamming shut against his head, trapping him there. Noah slides his hands under my ass and squeezes the soft flesh. Hard. I buck against his mouth as my orgasm drips out of me. The thought of marking him with my release is so filthy and yet such a turn on. I grind against him again, nearly losing my mind when he growls bites down on my clit.

The sting of his teeth followed by the smooth heat of his tongue has me coming again. The orgasm quickly rips through my body, leaving me breathless and unable to move once I come down.

Noah sets my legs down and then scoops me up, carrying me bridal style out of the room. I laugh softly and kick my legs out, peppering kisses along his jaw and neck until we get to my room.

He looks down at me with unbridled lust, which is only magnified when I see his mouth still glistening with my release. I don't stop to think about it, I just lean up and kiss him, tasting myself on his lips and moaning softly as he opens up for me.

One minute we're licking and kissing and devouring each other, and the next minute I'm falling through the air, only to land on the bed. Taking the hint, I sit up and whip my t-shirt over my head, so I'm only in my bra. Noah's eyes are wide, almost like a cartoon character. I giggle and then moan when Noah climbs on top of me and takes my lips in another wild kiss. I spread my legs for him, my bare pussy grinding against his jean-covered cock.

"Such a dirty fucking girl, aren't you, Jade?" Noah whispers as he drags his nose and lips down my throat and chest, placing a kiss in between my breasts.

"Only for you," I tell him truthfully. Noah looks up from in between my breasts, his eyes soft this time. I can tell he likes that he's my first everything. I like it too. "I want to see you too," I pout, hoping to finally get a glimpse at all those tasty muscles I just know he's hiding under his clothes.

Noah looks conflicted like he wants to be naked but also doesn't want to leave me for a single second. "Let me help," I offer, giving him what I hope is a sexy smile.

"That's the best damn idea I've heard in a long time, darlin'," he winks at me, leaning back when I push on his chest. Together, we stand and strip him out of everything until we're face to face, Noah in just his boxer briefs and me in just my bra. He reaches out and cups my breasts, then slides his hands to my back to undo the clasp.

"Wait," I whisper, my heart thudding uncontrollably in my chest. Noah freezes, his eyes searching mine to see what's wrong. "You first," I grin, eyeing his barely contained erection.

Noah smiles deviously and hooks his thumbs in the waistband of his underwear, pulling them down to reveal a goddamn log. I swear he's not real. I mean, what the *fuck*? He's massive, and...beautiful. I've never seen a dick in real life, and I certainly never thought I'd use that word to describe one, but there it is. His cock is gigantic, veined, throbbing, and jutting out right at me. He's hungry. For me. That thought has my thighs wet with my own hunger.

I feel Noah tap my chin with his finger, and I realize my mouth is literally hanging open at the sight of him. I snap my mouth closed and blush profusely. I'm sure I look like an idiot. Noah just chuckles and gives me a sweet kiss on my lips, my cheek, my jaw, and then his mouth ghosts over my ear. "Your turn," he murmurs, while his deft fingers pinch the clasp of my bra and undo it in one swift motion.

I step back and let my bra fall on the floor. I've never been naked in front of a man before, but the way Noah is looking at me doesn't leave any room for doubt. He's taking his time drinking all of me in, so I do the same.

Noah is gorgeous. Broad shoulders that have soaked up so many of my tears already, strong arms roped in muscles, defined pecs, and abs that flex as my eyes roam over his tanned skin. I allow myself a few more seconds of open gawking before trailing my gaze back up to meet his.

He smiles so tenderly at me, making me feel completely seen, completely safe, and completely sexy. It's a heady combination, one that makes me bolder than I've ever been. I reach out and place the palm of my hand on his chest, loving the way he shudders at my touch. Noah sighs and leans into me, then takes my other hand and places it on his chest as well, right over his heart. His hands cover mine, while we just stand and stare at each other. This is it. This is everything.

Noah leads me over to the bed and lays me down so gently before kissing his way up my body. I bite my lip and spread my legs wider for him, wanting more of his skin on my skin. Wanting to be connected to him in every single way. He settles his hips in between my legs, his hot and heavy cock laying across my slit.

He begins thrusting his hips, gliding his massive dick along my folds and gathering up my honey. My nerves sizzle and pop each time the head of his cock taps my swollen clit. I swear I could cum just from this, but Noah has other ideas.

The tip of his cock nudges in my entrance, only going in a fraction of an inch. Even so, my opening stretches to accommodate his size, a burning sensation tearing through my core and making my muscles tight.

"Relax, darlin'," Noah whispers into my lips before kissing me slowly. "I'm a big man, but I promise I'll go slow. I haven't been with anyone in almost a decade, never even thought about it, but you, sweet Jade..." he takes a deep, controlled breath. "You have destroyed me in the best way possible. I want to share everything with you, including this. Will you let me?"

The tears in my eyes aren't from pain but from an overwhelming sense of gratitude. This big, stubborn, sexy, sweet cowboy wants me in every single way. "Please," I whisper. "I want you to take me, Noah. All of me."

He presses his forehead to mine and eases in another inch. I no longer have a barrier, thanks to years of riding horses, but he's still stretching me so incredibly wide.

"Let me in, Jade. Open up for me and let me take care of you the way you deserve."

I feel myself relax at his words, my tight channel pulsing and sucking his huge length inside of me. Noah rubs his nose against mine and then thrusts forward, swallowing my cry by kissing the air out of my lungs. He breathes life into me as he sinks his thick dick into my body.

"Ohmygod, Noah, ohmygod..." I moan, crossing my ankles behind his back in an attempt to keep him there, so deep inside of me.

"Fuck," he grits out, burying his face in my neck and biting me there as he slowly withdraws himself. Noah slides back inside of me, going even further this time, filling me up to the absolute limit and then backing out again.

He grunts and snaps his hips, slamming home in one hard thrust. I choke on the scream in my throat and bow my back off of the mattress, clawing at his skin as he hammers in and out of me. Each time he hits the end of me, my body jerks as if being electrocuted.

"Don't...stop..." I breathe out as I cling to his trembling body.

"Not a fucking chance, darlin'," he growls, bending down to suck on one of my nipples. I'm shocked when the tingling sensation is mirrored in my clit, as if the two are connected by a string. Noah chuckles and bites my nipple, making me buck my hips and take him impossibly deeper. We both groan, getting lost in the way our bodies fit together. "Do you like that, Jade? Like when I bite your nipples and fuck this tight little pussy?"

"Oh, fuck...fuck yes," I moan, barely recognizing my own voice.

"Good girl," he grunts before sucking more of my breast into his mouth.

A delicious wave of pleasure courses through me when I hear those words. *Good girl.* I want to be good for him. I want him to love me the way I already love him. I want to please him and make him happy with me. I feel my pussy tighten around his dick at the thought of him saying it again.

Noah's thrusts become harder, faster, as he licks and nips his way up to my mouth. His lips are inches from mine. All I can think about is tasting him while he fucks me. Noah pounds into me and drags my bottom lip between his teeth, grinning when I whimper into his mouth.

"You want to be my good girl, Jade," he whispers huskily. I nod my head frantically, my pussy throbbing wildly as more of my cream drips out of me and soaks the sheets. "I feel you, baby, I fucking *feel* how much you want to cum. So do it, Jade, be a good girl, and cum all over me."

He kisses me as he slams into me in long, rough strokes. I'm stuffed so full of his cock I can't take a full breath. I unhook my ankles from behind him and place my feet flat on the bed so I can meet him thrust for thrust.

"Christ, you feel incredible. Now cum for me, cum for me right the fuck now, Jade."

I scream as my orgasm burns through me, all of my muscles spasming at once in the most intense moment I've ever experienced. My blood feels like sharp razor blades coursing through my veins, the pain spiking my pleasure into heights unknown.

"So goddamn beautiful, coming for me like a goddess," he grunts, fucking me through my orgasm and then leaving me completely.

I almost cry at the loss of him, but Noah just grabs my hips and flips me over, tugging me back so I'm on all fours. I gasp as he enters me in one hard thrust, his thighs smacking against my ass as he bottoms out, hitting me so incredibly deep.

"Noah!" I moan, arching my back and wedging his thick dick even deeper inside of me. He taps some super-sensitive spot, making my pussy convulse and my limbs shake.

"There it is," he grunts in satisfaction, gripping my hips and digging his fingers into my soft flesh. He bounces me off his cock, hitting that spot over and over, fucking me mercilessly until I'm coming again with his name on my lips. Noah holds still, his cock buried inside of me as my orgasm washes over me in violent waves. "Such a good girl. Give me one more, Jade, I need you to cum again for me."

I whimper and squeeze my walls around his hard cock, unable to give him any words at the moment. My body is deliciously sore and used, my pussy is swollen and sensitive, and I don't think I can take anything else, but I want to give Noah everything he wants.

One of his hands traces up my back, and then tangles in my hair. He tugs my head to the side and then leans down to kiss me as he slowly begins moving in and out of my tight channel. I feel his abs tense and flex against my ass as he works his fat cock in and out of me.

I press back against him as he surges forward, earning me a sexy growl from Noah. "That's it, baby, fuck me back, show me how much you want it."

I fist the sheets in my hands and rock back into Noah, swallowing his hard shaft in my pussy again and again. He grabs my breasts, kneading them and holding on to me while rutting into me savagely. Noah pinches my nipples and slams into me, each thrust pushing me closer and closer to the edge, his monster cock stretching me wider still.

"I'm...I'm..." I pant and gasp for air, barely hanging on to my sanity as he ravages my body and rips me open in powerful strokes.

"Let go, Jade, let go for me," he rumbles. "I'm right there with you, but I need you to cum first, so cum for me, sweetheart, cum all over my cock," he roars, shooting his hot cum deep inside of me.

My world erupts in pure bliss, my vision tunneling until I can't see, I can only feel. Pure light and energy are wrung from my very core as I twist in on myself and then go completely limp.

When I come to, I'm wrapped up in Noah's arms and he's placing sweet kisses all over my face. I giggle and scrunch my nose up, trying to get away from him. He just holds me tighter and rubs his nose against mine.

"You okay, darlin'?" He whispers.

"I'm so good, Noah. That was..." I blow out a breath, unable to find the right word to describe it.

"For me too, Jade. It was..." He pauses and then blows out a breath too.

"Exactly," I agree, and then laugh softly.

We lay there, a mess of tangled limbs and drying sweat, breathing the same air and snuggling in the afterglow. If I didn't know before, I definitely know now... I love Noah. I feel safe, wanted, beautiful, and fearless. It's that last one that has me opening my mouth and putting words to my most closely held secret.

"My daddy was a cheat with a vicious temper," I whisper.

Chapter 8

Noah

Jade's words shock me as much as they pain me. I've known ever since I first saw her at the funeral that something was off about their relationship. However, I never expected that Jim Rivera, town golden boy, handsome do-gooder, single father, and successful ranch owner had such skeletons in his closet. Then again, the successful ranch owner part was obviously a facade, so it shouldn't be surprising that the rest of his image was just as fake.

Not that I need any evidence for me to believe Jade. I've spent enough time with her to see the effects of her childhood, the way she apologizes for no reason, the tension and conflict that spring into her eyes whenever she talks about her dad, and of course the fact that she's been gone for four years.

Jim was a fair boss, seemed like a good enough guy most of the time. I couldn't quite get a read on him sometimes, but he never caused me any trouble.

Had I known the kind of man he was, I would have...what? Beat him? Run him out of town? I don't fucking know, but I feel like I should have done something. And then there's the speculation about his suicide...

"Everyone thinks he's this martyr, you know?" Jade whispers, bringing me back to the present. I tighten my hold on her and play with her hair, hoping to provide some sort of comfort while she says whatever she needs to say.

"My mom left him after she caught him cheating for the third time. Or maybe fourth time, I don't remember," she continues. "I actually was the one who found him, though thankfully both he and the other woman were done and mostly clothed when I accidentally walked in on them." Jade shivers in my arms, though I'm not sure if it's from a chill or from the memory. Either way, I pull the blankets up over us and tuck her into my side to give her more of my warmth.

"How old were you, sweetheart?"

"Eight. I remember sitting at the top of the stairs listening to Momma and Daddy fight about it. She said she was done being his picture-perfect wife while he brought other women into their home and then paid them to keep silent. He snarled at her and said she'd never have the balls to leave, especially with me still so young. I don't know who threw what or how it all started, but it sounded like a tornado blew through the house as they broke dishes and flipped furniture. I know dad landed a few blows as well as received his fair share of punches and scratches from mom. They weren't ever like that before, it was all passive-aggressive comments and bottled up, tension-filled silence up until then."

Her fragile voice trails off as if lost in that terrible memory. I can just picture a frightened little Jade huddled up on the stairs, listening in horror as her life crashed down around her, almost literally.

"I'm so sorry, Jade. That must have been awful," I whisper, kissing the top of her head.

She nods against my chest and takes a deep breath. "Momma left that night. She didn't bother to say goodbye, but when I woke up the next morning, I knew she was gone. I also knew I'd never see her again. It was just this feeling in my gut, and so far, I've been right," she sighs. "The next day, my dad was going on about how Momma had a mental breakdown and lashed out at him when he tried to help her. He told anyone who would listen that she ran off with another man, abandoning her child and leaving him alone with the responsibilities of a single-parent and a ranch owner."

"You never told anyone differently?" I ask, hoping to understand her better, not accuse her of anything.

Jade shrugs. "For a while, I think I believed his version of the truth. Even though I witnessed evidence to the contrary. The way he talked with such conviction about mom's mental health and how he insisted she was a master manipulator overshadowed my personal experience. But it wasn't long before he showed his true colors again. I guess all that anger that he had towards my mom had to come out somehow, so he figured he'd direct it at me."

I swallow down my own anger towards a man I worked alongside for years and yet never really knew. "Did he hurt you, baby?" I ask, trying to make my voice soft for her despite growing rage boiling up inside of me.

"He didn't hit me or anything like that," she assures me, allowing some of the tension to drain from my mind and body. "He got aggressive a few times, I guess. He was mainly an intimidator. He'd scream, hurl insults, straight up lie to my face, daring me to call him out. I tried figuring out what triggered his anger or what made him happy, but even up until the moment I walked out, I could never figure out how to please him."

Jade takes a cleansing breath before continuing.

"It all became too much. His public image versus the man behind closed doors. Walking on eggshells all the time, never knowing which version of Jim I'd get that hour. I remember staying up for days at a time when I was in middle school because for some reason he became obsessed with cleaning. He'd burst into my room at two in the morning and we'd have to clean every inch of the house. Nothing was ever good enough, and even when it was, I knew it was just a matter of time until Dad changed his mind."

"I understand why you left. I'm proud of you for getting yourself out of that situation, but I hate that I was here during your senior year and never knew any of that was going on." I lean back a bit and tip her chin up, staring into those brave, bold, bright green eyes of the woman I love. I want her to see that I've never meant anything more. It physically hurts to know we were practically living under the same roof while she was being emotionally abused and gaslighted by her dad.

Jade gives me a watery smile and rubs her nose up and down mine in our own little sign of affection. "I don't think I would have admitted to anything even if you saw something and confronted me about it. I had enough people tell me I was being an ungrateful brat to last a lifetime, and truth be told..." She trails off, her face blushing a pretty pink as she scrunches up her cute little nose. "Truth be told, I didn't want someone as handsome as you to call me a liar, or worse, feel sorry for me."

I quirk my lips up to the side at her little admission that she found me attractive even back then, but it does little to soothe the ache in my chest from not being there for her. I press my lips to her forehead and breathe in her sweet peaches and cream scent, mixed with a bit of sweat and sex. Needless to say, the smell makes me hard in an instant, though I tilt my hips away from Jade so she doesn't see. This isn't the time for that, however much my body protests.

"Well I don't think you're a liar, and I don't feel sorry for you," I tell her.

"You don't?"

God, her big round eyes, pink cheeks, and freckles all stare back at me, reminding me of how young and vulnerable she is. "Not at all. I believe every word, Jade. You're no liar. You're a fighter. A survivor. You did what you had to do, and then you came back here to face the music when the time came. That took a lot of courage, sweetheart. Knowing all of this about you doesn't make me pity you, it makes me stand in awe of your strength and beauty."

Jade buries her face in my chest right as the first tears fall. I hold her, rocking my sweet girl back and forth and whispering soothing words in her ear.

"I didn't come back soon enough though," she finally says, lifting up her head to look at me.

"What do you mean?"

"Well...what if...what if the insurance agent is right? What if he committed suicide?"

I take a deep breath and try to figure out how to answer her, though honestly, I've been wrestling with that uncomfortable fact ever since she told me.

"First of all, insurance companies are always looking for a way out of handing over checks, so we should take their assessment with a grain of salt. But more importantly, you need to know that your father's actions are his own. That includes how he treated you and your mom. None of that shit was your fault, baby. Even if you acted out like any kid does from time to time, your parents should have been there to discipline you in a loving way, not an intimidating way. You should have had a safe place to grow up and make mistakes, and I'm so sorry that you didn't."

Jade bites her lip nervously and tries to look away from me. I grip her chin lightly between my thumb and forefinger, making sure she hears me and sees me as I tell her this next part.

"Jade, your dad's death is not your fault. If, and that's a big *if*, he took his own life, it was because a lifetime of demons caught up with him. It sounds like he probably had an undiagnosed mental or mood disorder thrown into the mix as well."

She tears up and tries again to pull away from me, but I don't let her.

"As hard as that is to hear, sweet girl, it's the truth. Were there signs that those of us closest to him could have been more aware of? Maybe. I know that question will haunt me for a long time. But the thing is, Jim never asked for help. He had to have known his behavior wasn't normal, wasn't healthy, and certainly wasn't good for you, his own daughter. But he was unwilling to change, unwilling to heal. That's why I'm so goddamn proud of you, Jade, for wanting to be better. For wanting to heal. We're all broken, and sometimes that means we love from a broken place. But those of us willing to do the work of pushing through that pain come out the other side whole and able to accept as well as give the love we need."

Tears spill down her delicate face, but she's smiling at me. "How did you get so wise?" she teases, kissing my nose.

I pull her close and kiss her lips tenderly, with all the love in my heart. "Let's just say I've had to fight through my fair share of shit too, darlin'," I wink at her before going in for another kiss. Jade, however, pulls back and presses a finger to my lips, making me frown.

"Oh, no, mister. You're not getting off the hook that easily. I told you things I've never told anyone before, so now you gotta tell me about this shit you had to fight through. Fair is fair," she raises one eyebrow so saucily it makes me want to roll her on her back and fuck that smug look off her face and replace it with one of pure rapture.

Instead, I settle back down and tuck her into my side once again.

"It's an old tale, really. My parents never understood why I wanted to work with horses instead of getting a *normal* job and make a shit ton of money like they did. They set me up with a friend's daughter in hopes we'd settle down, pop out a few kids and live their outdated version of the American dream. My ex thought she could change me, make me want to move to the city and have an excitin' life, but I was content with working outdoors. I knew I'd never survive in the city. I did everything I could to prove to my ex that life on the ranch could be fulfilling in a way other kinds of work never would be. Long story short, she cheated on me with her boss and then left me for the bastard. My parents were upset that I wouldn't give her a second chance, which put a strain on that relationship as well. They still update me on her sometimes, as if I give a shit. Last I heard, she married her boss, divorced him, and married another, richer, more connected man. They live in Dallas. Dodged a bullet there, but it hurt all the same."

"She's a fucking fool!" Jade spits out, all fiery and ready to jump to my defense. Yeah, my dick grows harder at her conviction and feisty attitude.

"We both were. I thought I loved her and that our love would overcome whatever obstacles were in our way."

"But you didn't? Love her, that is?" Jade asks in a softer voice, such a contrast to the venom in her tone at the mention of my ex.

I roll Jade on top of me in one swift motion, guiding her legs to straddle me as she steadies herself on my chest. I cup the back of her neck and pull her down so her face is inches from mine.

"You're the only woman I've ever loved, Jade. Only you." I don't give her a chance to respond, I just take her lips in a possessive kiss, hoping to convey all the unspoken promises of forever. We get lost in each other, breaking and healing at the same time with every touch, every kiss, every soft moan.

Jade leans back and props herself up on her knees, positioning her soaking little pussy over my raging cock. Fuck, the way she's looking at me right now, her heart on display, her strength and desire shining through, her perky, perfect breasts, flat tummy, and thick, creamy thighs... Goddamn, this woman is mine, my forever, my precious, sexy as hell, future wife. The mother of my children. I feel it deep in my soul, the rightness settling in my bones and washing away everyone and everything that came before her.

Never breaking eye contact, Jade slowly slides down my hard shaft, engulfing me in her perfect, wet heat. I groan at the sight of my dick disappearing into her ripe little cunt, precum leaking out of the tip as I think about being inside of her every damn day from now until forever.

"Fuck, darlin', you got me so wrapped up in you," I tell her, my voice gravelly and laced with need.

When she's fully seated on me, we both take a moment to catch our breath. "Wrapped up in me, or wrapped up in my pussy?" she teases. Fuck, hearing the word *pussy* fall from her pouty lips makes my cock twitch. Jade gasps and instinctively rolls her hips, wedging me deeper inside of her.

"Why not both?" I growl, grabbing her hips and helping her find the perfect rhythm for both of us.

"Oh God, ohmygod..."

Jade curls her fingers into my chest, her nails digging into my flesh and making me grunt with pain and pleasure. She bounces up and down my cock, crying out and twisting her hips when the angle is just right to hit her G-spot.

"That's it, Jesus, that's so fucking it, beautiful. Use me up, darlin', fuck me until you cum all over my big dick, you got that?"

Jade moans in response, but that's not good enough for me. I spank her tight ass and grab her cheek hard. She gasps for air as her pussy chokes my cock. "Yes, yes, I want to cum all over you," she cries out.

She rocks back and forth in a desperate attempt to find relief. I reach out and cup her gorgeous tits, pinching her nipples and groaning as her whole body shivers on top of me. I keep one hand kneading and massaging her breasts while the other reaches between us and rubs her clit, causing her to tense and shout my name.

"I feel you, Jade, I know you want to cum for me," I growl.

Her thighs tighten around my hips, her pussy pulsing wildly as more of her sweet honey pours down over my dick. She takes in a huge breath of air and goes completely still.

And then she shatters all around me.

Jade squeezes my cock so fucking tightly it almost hurts as her orgasm ravages her tiny body. It's amazing watching her come completely undone for me. She's so fucking beautiful, shit, I never want to leave her snug little pussy. I never want to stop making her cum.

She collapses on my chest and buries her head in my neck, kissing and nipping at me as her hips continue to roll and stutter. I grab her ass and help her grind down on top of me until she cums again. I feel her orgasm spread throughout her body as I slide one hand up her back so I can tangle my fingers in her hair and pull her lips up to meet mine.

Jade moans into the kiss, driving me absolutely crazy with the way her tongue slides against mine. I flip us over and pound that pink little pussy with everything I have, swallowing her cries of ecstasy.

Leaning back, I throw one leg over my shoulder, and then the other, grabbing onto the headboard as I slam in and out of her. "Mine, fucking *mine*," I growl, looking into her eyes, branding her with my stare, my cock, and soon, my baby in her belly. "Fuck!" I roar, feeling my dick swell up inside of her.

"Noah, shit, oh shit, I'm..." Jade whimpers and claws at the sheets, thrashing her head back and forth.

"Cum for me, Jade, cum for me like a good girl."

Jade screams and lets go of every goddamn thing, snapping her pussy around me again and again as she's hit with never-ending waves of bliss. She's shivering and sweating and moaning uncontrollably.

With one last thrust, I burst inside of her, coming in long, powerful ropes, emptying every last drop into her fertile, young pussy. Goddamn, the vision of her round with our kid, her breasts full and sensitive... I release another round of hot cum deep inside of her before rolling off to the side and dragging her limp, sated body on top of mine.

Jade snuggles up next to me and kisses my chest, my neck, my jaw, and finally my lips. "I love you too," she whispers before kissing me deeply.

When we finally break apart, I pull the blankets over us once again and wrap her up in my arms. "Love you so fucking much, sweetheart," I whisper as I rub my nose up and down hers. I see her long lashes flutter and then she closes her eyes, tucking her head under my chin.

We fit so damn perfectly it makes my chest ache. Once I hear her soft snores, I finally allow myself to drift off to sleep as well.

Chapter 9

Jade

I shuffle and straighten and rearrange the papers in the folder I prepared for the bank. I figure the only option to get the money I need to save the ranch is to get a second mortgage on the place. And if that doesn't work, I'll try for a business loan. As a last resort, I'll see if I can take a personal loan, but my credit is less than stellar.

Noah has tried talking to me a few times over the last few days about giving me money to help out, but I always change the subject or just kiss him until both of us forget all about the ranch and the rest of the world. It's been a week since Noah and I made love for the first time, and I won't lie, aside from the impending doom of the ranch, life is perfect. I'm more determined than ever to fix the place up and make it home again. Or, rather, make it home for the first time.

I never thought I'd come back to this town, let alone try to settle down and make a life here. Noah asked me last night if I was okay living in the same house where I grew up. I struggled through the many emotions that crashed down on me, but like always, Noah gathered me up in his arms and soaked up my tears, finding another piece of my heart and healing me little by little.

After talking everything out, in between a few orgasms, of course, I realized I want to make new memories here. I love the ranch itself, and I didn't realize how much I missed it until I came back and filled my lungs with the earthy, clean air only found out here. Noah promised me we'd have new, wonderful memories of this place in no time. I told him I already have a few.

I didn't tell him, however, about my appointment at the bank today. I feel a little guilty, but I'm determined to do this on my own. What Noah and I have is so fragile still and it would absolutely ruin me if money got in the way of our relationship. I know Noah said I'm the only woman he's ever loved, but he also said he thought that once before about someone else. He thought their love would overcome, but it didn't. I want to make him happy and prove to him I'm capable of handling things.

"Ms. Rivera?" a portly woman in her fifties asks, stepping out into the lobby of the bank to address me.

"Yes, ma'am, that's me." I attempt a confident smile, but I'm sure she can see me shakin' in my boots.

"I'm Betty Kramer. Follow me into my office," she clips out while giving me a brief handshake. Her tone is professional, but a little bit curt. My stomach rolls, the nerves taking over despite my attempts to swallow them down.

Once we're both seated and I've been offered a variety of beverages that I turned down, Betty clears her throat and stares at me over her glasses. I can already tell she's made her decision, but I'm going to try like hell to get her to change her mind.

"Ms. Rivera, I've been looking over the state of Rivera Ranch, and I must say, I was surprised to find out about the financial situation. I'm sorry for your loss, by the way. Jim was a good man."

"Thank you," I respond automatically. Everyone I've run into in my short time here so far has some version of the same condolences. "I was surprised to find out about the ranch as well."

"Mmhmm, I'm sure you were," Betty says, giving me a pointed look. Great, another local who has already judged me. She probably blames me for my father's death too.

I take a cleansing breath, biting back all of the snarky things I want to say to her. I remind myself I'm here to make a good impression, not to reinforce whatever bullshit she thinks about me. "I suppose that brings us to why I'm here," I try to say in my most confident, professional voice. I'm not sure if I pulled it off, or if it matters even if I did.

"I'm sorry, Ms. Rivera. I don't think we'll be able to help you."

I swallow down the lump in my throat and press on. "If you could just do me the courtesy of looking over my business plan?"

Betty harrumphs but takes the folder from my outstretched hand. As she's skimming over the charts and budgets, I start to explain it to her since she's not reading a single word of what I prepared.

"As you can see, there are several ideas for additional revenue streams, we just need some money to jumpstart the place again. Renting out stables, buying up more cattle from local auctions, even transforming one of the old barns into a venue to host events like weddings and such. All that money will go back into the ranch to help with upkeep and hiring new staff. If you'll turn to page five, you'll see that I've charted out the potential profits over the next five years, including the increased property value."

She turns to page five, clucking her tongue and shaking her head slightly. She's not even open to the possibility of me being successful, but I continue on.

"I'm confident that I'll be able to turn things around, especially considering the loyal ranch hands and their valuable expertise."

Betty sighs and closes the folder. "Look honey, we can't possibly approve you for a second mortgage."

"What about a business loan?"

Betty shakes her head no.

"A personal loan, then?" I ask, grasping at straws.

"Jade, dear, in all honesty, there's no way you're qualified to take out a loan. I've looked at your credit score," she says with more than a little bit of judgment in her voice. "And you'll be hard-pressed to find any bank that will give you a loan, business, personal, or otherwise."

"Please, if you just hear me out, I have more ideas—"

"I'm sorry, there's nothing to be done about it."

"Really?" I ask, my anger and shame bubbling up to the surface. "It seems like there's a lot that can be done, as I've shown you in my business plan. I'm just asking for a few thousand—"

"A hundred thousand," Betty so helpfully corrects.

"Give me a chance," I plead, though I know it's no use.

"You have my final answer, and I assure you any other loan officer will tell you the same thing. It's not a good investment. Though, I will be sorry to see Rivera Ranch go under."

I shoot daggers at her as I stand up and grab my business plan off of her desk. "Well lucky for you, that won't be happening," I spit out. "I'm saving my ranch with or without you."

"Bless your little heart," Betty says. The classic Southern brush off. "I really hope you can make it work." She gives me a sympathetic smile, but I know it's all fake. She just wants to get me out of her office before I cause a scene.

I stomp out to my truck before I do any more damage. The last thing I need is to get another bad reputation around here.

I'm fuming behind the wheel of the old truck, pissed beyond belief that she didn't even give me a chance. I knew it would be an uphill battle, but deep down I had hoped the small-town camaraderie would win out. And if nothing else, the memory of good ol' Jim Rivera would pull at their heartstrings. But no. Seems their disdain for me is stronger than their love for my dad.

My knuckles turn white as I grip the steering wheel and pull out of the parking lot of the bank.

"Now what?" I ask the universe. If my projections are even a little bit accurate, the ranch won't survive the winter. Where will I go? Will Noah come with me wherever I end up? What if I have to move to a big city to find better job opportunities?

These doubts and questions swirl in my head and twist up my gut. I'm so caught up in my worries that I hadn't noticed the black sedan following close behind me. There's not much out this way once you get out of town, just a bunch of private property. Plus, that shiny new car sure ain't from around here.

My suspicion grows when I turn down the long dirt road that runs along the north side of the ranch. A feeling of dread comes over me and I hit the gas. The car speeds up too, which sends my pulse racing. Who the hell is following me? Is this the modern-day equivalent of the villagers running the monster out of town with torches and pitchforks?

I make a hard right on the narrow road leading up to the ranch, causing the truck to fishtail a bit on the loose gravel. I gain control of the vehicle and gun it again, needing to be in the safety of Noah's arms. I don't know what the fuck is going on, but there's a pit in my stomach and my heart is rattling around painfully inside of my chest.

The main house is in sight now, and I pull the truck right up into the front lawn, not even caring about the potential damage to the grass. I need to get as close to the front door as possible so I can lock myself inside.

As soon as I jump out of the truck, however, my worst nightmare steps out of the black sedan.

"Jade," Adam bites out. "You're one difficult woman to track down."

"Uh, uh, um…" I stutter out, my voice as shaky as my legs. I try running towards the front door, but stumble when my left knee decides to give out. Adam grabs my forearm and hauls me into his chest.

"Not so fast, I came all this way to see you, don't you at least want to hear me out?"

"What makes you think I'd want to talk to you after I ignored all of your calls and texts?" I say, the anger replacing my anxiety. Seriously, why won't he take a hint?

Adam's eyes grow fierce, glinting dangerously in the late afternoon light. He tightens his grip on my arm and shoves me up against his car, blocking me in with his body. I almost gag at the overpowering scent of his cologne.

"I'm willing to forgive you for this behavior. I heard your father passed away, so I'm sure you're taking your time to grieve, but the time is up. You're coming back to Denver with me," he grits out, his face turning red.

"You're delusional, Adam. I don't want to be with you, I've *never* wanted to be with you. I can't deal with your entitled, arrogant bullshit right now—"

His hand covers my mouth to prevent me from finishing my sentence. Terror pierces through me, puncturing my lungs and siphoning out all of my breath. I recognize the dark look overtaking his features. The same one my father had when he let the unhinged, vicious beast creep up and make decisions for him. The only way I know how to deal with it is to play nice until I can get away. Men like Adam, like my father, crave power, especially when they can take it from someone weaker than them.

"Shut that filthy whore mouth of yours and listen when I speak to you." He tightens his hold on my face and presses his body even further into mine, pinning me against the car. I whimper against his palm and swallow back tears. I don't want this psychopath to have the satisfaction of seeing me cry.

I wish I told Noah about the mess I left behind in Denver. I wish I told him about my appointment at the bank so he would know to look for me if I didn't show up for dinner. I wish I wasn't so prideful and just let him help me in the first place. I could've been out working the ranch with him when Adam showed up. I have no doubt Noah would protect me. As it is, he and the other ranch hands could be anywhere out on the property and probably wouldn't hear me even if I screamed at the top of my lungs.

"Shh, shh, now," Adam coos, dropping his hand from my mouth and petting my head instead. It's not comforting like when Noah does it. No, Adam's touch is controlling, condescending even, like I'm his dumb pet that doesn't know any better than to act out. "I just want what's best for you, you understand, don't you Jade?"

To the outside observer, it might seem like he's being sweet and caring, but the twitch in his left eye gives his words a much more sinister undertone.

I just nod my head, opting for compliance in an attempt to earn his trust. If I can get him to agree to let me go inside under the guise of packing up my things, maybe I can grab my phone and call Noah.

"Good, that's good. I'm glad you're starting to see things my way." Adam strokes my cheek, his boney, cold fingers sending chills down my spine. He trails his hand down my throat, wrapping it around my neck in a light but firm grip. It's the promise of violence if I don't submit. The reminder of his power over me. "This worn-down ranch is a lost cause. You deserve the finest clothes, a penthouse suite, parties and champagne, and lavish vacations. That's what I can give you. Don't you want me to take you away from this dump?"

He doesn't wait for my response before pulling me forward by my neck and forcing his tongue into my mouth. I try twisting away from him, but he has one of my arms trapped between my body and the car, and the other still in his punishing grip. I bite his tongue, but that only seems to spur him on. The barely contained tears spill over my cheeks and I can't take a breath. He's suffocating me with his hand on my neck and his mouth over mine.

Noah, please, please save me...

Chapter 10

Noah

I can't believe it. I'm watching Jade kiss another man with my own two eyes, but I still can't process that information. Neither one of them saw me when I opened the front door and started walking towards them.

Jade said she had some errands to run in town and didn't know how long she'd be. I offered to come with her and then take her out to a nice dinner, but she said I should probably be out on the ranch since it's Cory's day off and Isaiah is getting over a stomach bug. I was going to fight her on it but decided this was one of those moments where I needed to accept her order as the boss. I don't ever want her to feel like I'll override her decisions in regard to the ranch or use our relationship as a way to manipulate her. So, I reluctantly let her go.

If I only knew she was traipsing off to meet with some douchebag city slicker asshole, I would have insisted on coming with her to try and convince her otherwise.

Memories of my ex and her equally as horrible douchebag, city slicker of a man race through my head and cloud my vision, making me clench my fists in anger. I can't watch the same thing happen to me again, so I turn around and head back towards the house.

I heard what he said about Jade deserving the best. She nodded her head, completely under his spell. He told her about the fancy, extravagant lifestyle he could give her, and Jade must have smiled in that bright way of hers, because in the next second, they were sucking face.

Shame, rage, embarrassment, and overwhelming sadness wash over me making my brain all fuzzy and my muscles twitch with the need to put my fist through a fucking wall.

But then I hear it.

A strangled, gut-wrenching sound.

Every single thought and feeling disappears, replaced with the need to get to my Jade. I turn around and see her struggling against the lanky but tall man in an impeccable suit. He has a hand around her neck and he's snarling insults right in her face while Jade tries to turn her head away from him.

Jade's green eyes are filled with terror, and I want to fucking punch my own goddamn face for doubting her. If I got to her sooner...

I can't think about that right now, I just have to save her and murder the fucker who hurt her. Jade's eyes go wide and flash with hope when she looks over the asshole's shoulder and sees me coming.

Grabbing the man by the collar of his expensive suit, I rip him away from my Jade and throw him on the ground.

"Hey, what the fuck?!" he screams.

I don't answer him with words, but rather with my fist cracking against his nose. I hear it snap and then a satisfying stream of blood spills down his face. Again and again, I beat this motherfucker into the ground with my fists, until I feel tiny hands pounding on my back.

"Noah," Jade sobs. Her voice is strained and pleading. "You're gonna kill him. You can't go to prison, I need you here," she begs me.

I throw my fist back one more time but stop myself when I'm an inch from his face. The coward winces. I spit in his face and give him a kick in the stomach for good measure before turning around and gathering Jade up in my arms.

She's trembling and sobbing and gasping for air as I scoop her up and cradle her against my chest. Jacob and Isaiah must have heard the commotion, their eyes wide as they approach us and take in the scene.

"Jacob, tie up this degenerate, none too carefully, you hear?" I bark out. "Isaiah, call the cops and let me know when they arrive. I'm taking Jade inside."

Both men nod and get to work. I'm thankful that they seem to know not to ask questions right now.

Once inside the house, I gently set Jade down on the couch and drape a blanket around her. She's crashing from the adrenaline rush, shaking and white as a ghost. I can tell Jade is in shock by the blank look in her eyes, but I know soon enough it will all hit her. I just pray she can forgive me for letting that fucker touch her.

I head to the kitchen and fill up a glass with water before grabbing the bottle of Aspirin. As soon as the adrenaline leaves her body, she's going to be sore. I rush back over to her and encourage her to take the pills and have a few sips of water. She obeys me without hesitation even though her eyes are unfocused and staring straight ahead.

Sitting down next to her, I contemplate whether to hold her or give her space. I want nothing more than to wrap her up in my arms and never let her go, but I don't want to crowd her or touch her when she's still so fragile and in shock.

Jade doesn't let me wrestle with my decision for long, however. She turns to me with unshed tears in her eyes, her bottom lip trembling and barely containing a heartbreaking whimper. Jade leans into me, and I pull her into my lap and cover her with my body, my strength, my love.

"I'm so sorry," she squeaks out. It just about breaks me apart to hear her apologizing to me, but I have to be strong for her right now.

"Jade, none of this is your fault. I don't know the history you two have, but there's never, *ever* an excuse to lay hands on a woman or force her to do anything she's uncomfortable with. Do you understand me, sweetheart?"

She nods into the side of my neck, her warm tears wetting my skin and ripping my heart to shreds.

There's a knock on the door and then Isaiah enters. He immediately takes his hat off and holds it to his chest as a sign of respect for Jade. "Can I let the officers in, Jade?"

Jade looks up at me as if to get my permission.

"It's your decision, darlin'. Are you up for it? If not, I'll take you down to the station tomorrow after things settle down."

Jade nods and looks over at Isaiah. "I'm ready. I just want this all to be over."

"Yes, ma'am," Isaiah says, opening the door and nodding for the officers to come in while I set Jade down next to me instead of on my lap.

A male and female officer walk in and introduce themselves to us. Officer Espinoza, the female officer, gently asks Jade if she can tell them everything she knows about the guy outside - whose name is apparently Adam. Jade looks up at me, her big, green eyes full of worry.

"It's okay, darlin'," I encourage her. She grabs my hand and squeezes it like she's trying to keep me in place. There's no way in hell I'd leave her side right now, possibly ever, so she has nothing to worry about.

"I'm sure you already know that my father passed away recently," Jade starts. Both officers nod and offer their condolences. "The same day I got the call about his death, I was fired and kicked out of my apartment," she says all in a rush.

I'm shocked, not only at all of the horrible, life-altering events that happened at the same time for her but the fact that she didn't tell me. I won't lie, it stings a bit that she felt like she couldn't share everything with me, but it's not about that right now. The room has gone silent, and when I focus my attention back on Jade, I see it's because she's looking up at me apologetically.

"Adam was my boss," she continues, turning her head away from me and slipping her hand out of mine. I feel like a lead weight was dropped on my stomach, but I try to keep myself together. She won't even look at me, and that hurts more than anything else.

"Why do you think he followed you out here?" Officer Espinoza asks.

I sit and listen as Jade tells the officers about how she got a job as a receptionist at a PR firm when she first moved out to Denver. Soon, she was promoted to secretary, which had been her job for the last few years. Jade shifts uncomfortably and then tells us how she was called into Adam's office recently and given a huge promotion and a raise out of the blue. Adam the asshole apparently thought Jade would be so thankful, she'd fuck him. The thought has me choking down rage. Jade takes a deep breath and gets the rest of it out.

"He called me up to his office one day, a few weeks after my promotion. He tried kissing me, but I fought him off. Kicked him in the nuts and slapped him," Jade says with more than a little pride. "He fired me on the spot. I was all too happy to get out of his office, but I ran into my co-worker and roommate, Jen, in the hallway. I knew Jen had a crush on Adam, but I guess the two of them were sleeping together and she thought I was jealous and seduced Adam or something. Long story short, her name was on our apartment lease, not mine, so I lost a job, a home, and a dad in one fell swoop," she finishes, laughing without humor and then shivering a bit.

"Has he been in contact with you since you've been out here?" the officer asks.

Jade nods, which makes my chest tighten painfully. What the fuck? First, I didn't know about her dad while she was living here, and now this? How can I protect her if she doesn't talk to me? My blood is surging through my veins and I clench my fists at my sides. I'm not angry with Jade, I'm more confused and frustrated that the stubborn woman I love doesn't trust me. I'm fucking pissed at Adam, at Jim, at anyone and everyone that broke Jade's trust and made her fearful.

I look over at Jade again and see that she's inching away from me. The thought of her being afraid of me slices right through my thoughts, leaving a searing pain behind. I would never, ever forgive myself if she thought for even one second that I would hurt her. I take a few calming breaths and brace myself for what's next.

"I had my phone turned off for the first few days I was out here. When I turned it back on, I had a bunch of missed calls and texts from him. He seemed sort of all over the place, some were apologetic, some were mean, but I never thought he'd do something like this. I just wanted to forget anything happened." Jade finally looks over at me, her eyes brimming with tears again. "I just wanted to forget," she whispers again to me, offering an explanation for why she didn't tell me sooner.

I reach out and take her hand again, kissing her palm and then twining our fingers together so she won't pull her hand away again.

The officers ask her a few more questions and then I give them my side of things. Before long, they are heading back outside, where Jacob and Isaiah have been watching Adam. "We've got it from here, boys," I hear the male officer say before I close the door behind him.

Walking back over to Jade, I see her all curled up on the end of the couch. I fucking hate today.

"It's over now, sweetheart," I tell her softly as I sit down next to her and pull her back into my lap. "I've got you, darlin', I'm not going anywhere. You're safe right here," I whisper as I rock her back and forth.

"Noah, I swear I don't want him. I never wanted him. I'm not like your ex—"

"Shh, baby, don't even finish that thought."

"But—"

"Jade, stop," I tell her a little more harshly than I meant to. She stiffens in my arm and I want to punch myself in the face for about the fifth time today. Instead, I tuck some of her hair behind her ear and rest my forehead on hers. "Sorry, I'm just... Sorry, baby. I'm all over the place right now, but I'm not mad at you. You did nothing wrong, not then, not now."

I lift my head and press my lips to her forehead, breathing in her calming, familiar peaches and cream scent. Cupping the back of her neck, I hold her in place so she's looking right at me for this next part.

"Sweetheart..." God, how do I even begin to apologize to her? "I need to ask for your forgiveness." Jade furrows her brow, but I keep going, needing to get it all out now that I've started. "I was in the house when you pulled up. I came outside right before that fucker kissed you, and for a brief second, I thought..." I look away from her, shaking my head in disgust at my actions. Or, rather, my lack of actions.

"I swear, that's not—"

"Believe me, I know. I think I knew it then, I was just shocked. But, Jade, I... Fuck, I freaked out, I had a complete lapse of judgment and I walked away from you." I feel Jade's soft little hand cup my cheek and turn my head towards her. I don't see betrayal or hatred in her eyes. I see only understanding and forgiveness. "I fuckin' left you," I say, my voice cracking at the end. "I'm so sorry. If I would have beat that piece of shit the moment I laid eyes on him, I could have spared you from the worst of his attack."

"Noah, I don't blame you at all. You saved me from so much. Not only from Adam, but from my grief. You're helping me untangle the knot of emotions brought on by everything. I truly don't know how I would have survived this long back home without you."

"Sweetheart..." Her words mean every fucking thing to me, but Jade continues to amaze me with her sensitive and forgiving heart by brushing her lips against mine in the whisper of a kiss. Jade nuzzles her head into the crook of my shoulder and I hold her close, letting the rhythm of her heart and the warmth of her skin ground me.

I don't know how long we stay like that, but eventually, I feel Jade stir in my arms. I reluctantly let her go, and she stands up, holding out her hand to me. "Come take a shower with me?" She asks, biting her lip nervously.

Instead of taking her hand, I stand and scoop her up in my arms, smiling when she giggles. "Darlin', I love that sound," I murmur before kissing her nose and heading towards the bathroom upstairs.

Once inside, I close the door, turn on the water, and begin stripping us out of our clothes. I have a desperate need to feel her skin against mine and feel every inch of her beneath my fingertips. When we're both naked, Jade steps forward and cups my face in both of her hands, pulling me down so we're mere inches apart.

"I need to feel you, please make everything go away until it's just us. Please?"

"I love you, Jade." I breathe the words into her mouth before kissing her with all of my sorrow and strength.

She drops her hands from my face to my neck, holding on tight and deepening our kiss. I press us closer together, feeling her soft curves pour into the slats of my muscles. I pick her up with one arm under her waist and carry her into the warm water, pinning her against the tiled wall. Our lips never part, our kiss growing more desperate by the second.

Jade wraps her legs around me, her hands trickling over my arms, my chest, around my neck down my back. My tongue rakes across the roof of her mouth and she shivers against me, pressing up against my body as I wrap my fingers around the curls of her bright red hair. I want to hear more of her. Have more of her. Taste more of her.

Jade rolls her hips, brushing her wet little cunt against my raging hard dick. She moans into my mouth, causing me to jerk my hips and hit her clit.

"God, yes," she whimpers, spurring me on.

With a contained roar, I thrust forward, her mouth opening in a silent scream as I split her open in one, hard stroke. I slide back and into her again, this time swallowing her desperate cries until her hands slide to my back and score my flesh. Her hips press forward, taking another few inches until I'm bound to her, root to tip, as her pussy practically chokes me at the base.

"You feel so good, baby. Like coming home," I whisper into the shell of her ear before kissing down her neck.

Jade bows her back off the wall and presses her tits forward, practically begging me to suck on them, which I do, hungrily. I take her breast into my mouth, licking her pebbled nipple and grazing my teeth over her soft flesh, loving the way she shudders in my arms and drips more of her sweet juices down my dick.

I feel her tight little pussy flutter around me, her breath growing shallow as her chest rises and falls rapidly. Jade's muscles tense and her pussy gushes for me, throbbing around my cock as her body tightens and squeezes me, hurting me so fucking good.

I piston in and out of her, building her up, up, up, tapping her clit with the base of my cock on every stroke. "That's it, sweet Jade, cum for me, baby, cum for me and show me you're mine, only mine," I growl into the side of her neck before licking a line up to her jaw and nipping her there.

She goes still in my arms, her body wrapped around mine while her head tips back and her mouth hangs open. I lean over her, hovering my open mouth above hers right as her orgasm ravishes her tiny, soft body. I breathe in her little whimpers and moans that come with every wave of pleasure.

Her nails dig into my shoulders, making me grunt and thrust inside of her so fucking hard, once, twice, three times, and I bury my head in the side of her neck as I empty myself inside of her still-convulsing cunt.

I continue to rock in and out of her, prolonging our pleasure as long as possible. Jade shudders and jerks and then knots her pussy around my thick dick as she fucking cums again. I hold her shivering body up and keep her pressed against the wall, in absolute awe of this goddess in my arms.

Gently, I pull out of her and set her down on the floor, pulling her into my chest and kissing the top of her head. Silently, I grab the body wash, pour some in my hand, and massage the soap into every inch of her body. I knead away the tension in her back and shoulders, and then wash her hair, marveling at its color and texture. Every single thing about her is perfect.

When I'm done, Jade soaps me up and lets her hands wander over my body, like she's admiring me too. We rinse off and I wrap her up in a fluffy towel and carry her off to bed, where I crawl in next to her and turn so we're face to face.

"Can you tell me where you went today, sweetheart?" I ask quietly.

Shame flashes in her beautiful green eyes. "I went to the bank to try to get a loan," she whispers, not meeting my gaze. "I'm sorry, Noah, I'm so sorry. I was stupid. I just wanted you to know I'm not always such a burden, that I can take care of myself. I wanted you to be proud of me."

Jesus. I don't even know where to start with all of that. I'm in actual, physical pain that she thinks I'm not proud of her. I tip Jade's chin up and rub my nose up and down hers. She seems to relax a bit, a slight blush covering her cheeks. God, she's still so sweet. After everything we just did in the shower, it's this little gesture that undoes her. I want her to feel this loved every second of every day.

"Jade, I'm not your dad. I'm not going to fly off the handle if you tell me something upsetting. I'm not going to punish you cruelly or change the rules on you. I'm here to support you, to be your biggest fan, your most loyal friend. I want to protect you from every bad thing in this world, but you gotta talk to me and be honest about everything."

She nods, a few tears sliding down her face. I kiss them away and continue.

"And, sweetheart...I'm so goddamn proud of you. I told you before, but I'll tell you, again and again, however many times you need to hear it. I'm proud of you for knowing when you needed to leave here. I'm proud of the hard work you've done while you were away, and I'm so damn proud to see you fighting through the mess of demons and emotions since you've been back. Promise me, baby, promise me that you'll never doubt how deeply and reverently I love you."

Jade nods again, sighing deeply as I hold her close. I feel more than hear her whisper how much she loves me.

I know without asking how the meeting at the bank went, so I don't make her say it. Instead, I roll onto my back and tuck her into my side. She rests her head over my heart while I comb my fingers through her wet hair.

"My offer is still on the table, darlin'. Before you refuse me again, let me just say that I have the money. I've had enough money to buy my own ranch for a while now, and that was always the goal. I was waiting for the love of my life to come and run it with me. Now that I have you, sweetheart, I'm not letting you go. Whatever you want to do, be it save Rivera Ranch, or start over someplace new, I'm here to support you. My money, my heart, my fuckin' soul is all yours. All of me belongs to you."

Jade nods again, smiling into my chest.

"I take that as I yes?" I tease.

Propping herself up on one elbow, she looks me right in the eyes with determination and fire. Good. I needed to know she still had it in her after everything that happened.

"I'll take your heart and soul, but you have to take mine," she says. I'm about to agree and kiss the fuck out of that candy-sweet mouth of hers, but she stops me by placing a finger over my lips. "As for the money...I have a business plan. I want you to look it over and give me your honest feedback. I'll know if you're lyin' cuz you have a terrible poker face," she says, quirking one eyebrow up. I love this woman with everything that I am.

I nibble on her finger and then suck it into my mouth. Jade gasps and then giggles, pulling her hand away from me and dragging her wet finger down my chest. I groan and cup the back of her neck, drawing her down for a kiss.

When we break for air, I tuck her back into my side and guide her head so it's over my heart again, needing her closeness right now. "I'll look at your business plan, but I'm told I can be a stubborn old bastard, especially when it comes to the right thing. And giving you everything you want? Well, darlin', that's about the best thing there is."

Jade sighs dramatically and playfully slaps my chest. I grab her hand and flip her on her back so I can tickle her. She giggles and thrashes, and then curls up in my arms. We drift off to sleep, talking about the future and dreaming of our life together.

Chapter 11

Jade

The last three months have flown by. Noah and I discussed the business plan, and he even had a few helpful tweaks. The fact that he truly listened to what I had to say and read through everything with me made me love him even more. We came up with a list of goals for the ranch and began prioritizing which projects should be done first.

It's been a grueling couple of months working on repairs and hiring contractors and seasonal help, but the investment is already paying off. After repairs to the stables and cattle feeder, we began renting out the empty stalls and expanded the herd of cattle.

The next project was to clear out one of the old barns and use it as an event venue. I'm so excited with how everything is turning out. We're three weeks into the renovation, and things are moving along quickly. The construction crew estimates the final touches will be done next week.

After Noah and I discussed everything and decided to continue working on Rivera Ranch instead of starting over somewhere new, I still had a few doubts about being the town outcast. Sure, I don't go into town all that often, but still. As it turns out, once I decided to stay and word got around that I'm fixing up the place and making it even better, folks seemed more willing to hear me out.

Of course, I didn't go into any details about why I left, I just let them come to their own conclusions. That alone was a big step for me. I always thought if I ever came back, I'd tell every single judgmental person what kind of man my dad was. But when the opportunity arose, I found I didn't want to take away from their memory of Jim. What good would it do other than tarnishing his image and garnering me pity? Or worse, they might not believe me. There have been a few people who took the time to actually talk to me and thoughtfully inquire about the past. It's still hard to trust their kindness, but I'm working on letting people in.

I've had several calls already asking about when we'll be available to host events. People are booking the ranch several months in advance and paying a hefty deposit to secure their spot. Noah and I decided to use that money to hire a new cook. The two of us have been sharing that duty, and while I enjoy cooking, Noah convinced me that my skills and time can be better used elsewhere.

I put out an ad online and took one out in the local paper. So far, I have ten people who have applied, and three people I'm strongly considering. I almost narrowed the pool down to just two, but I kept being drawn to this other application The girl just turned eighteen, she has no professional cooking experience nor any references. Her resume says she loves cooking and food and promises she's up for the challenge of life on the ranch. It's the last line of her cover letter that kept bugging me and convinced me to give her a phone interview.

I know my resume is lacking, but I promise no one will work harder, with as much passion as I will.

There's just something about the tone, how she worded it, the overall feeling of her application that tugs at something deep inside of me. She's a desperate eighteen-year-old from L.A. who's looking for a fresh start in a new state. God knows I can relate to that.

She's the first up on my list of applicants to call. I promised Noah I'd make the final decision today. I've never conducted an interview before, so I have a LinkedIn article pulled up on the computer to help me out. Thank god for google, right? I tap the girl's number into my phone and hit the call button. I don't know why I'm nervous. I'm the one she has to impress, after all, but I just get this feeling like I'll have to handle her with care.

The phone rings twice, and then I hear someone on the other line take a huge breath before speaking.

"H-hello?" the shaky, timid voice asks. Then she clears her throat and tries again. "I mean, this is Teagan, are you calling from Rivera Ranch?" She's much more confident this time, but I still hear the fear in her voice. It's then that I know I'm going to hire her. But, might as well do the phone interview and give her the details about her new job.

"Yes, hi, Teagan, I'm Jade Rivera, owner of Rivera Ranch."

"Oh, wow, I didn't think you'd call me yourself," she says, bringing a smile to my face.

"Well, we're not a very big operation yet, just me, the foreman, and four ranch hands. But, we're investing more in the ranch and hoping to expand in the next year. Right now, your responsibilities would include breakfast, which is served at five every morning, and dinner, which is promptly at six. Lunch is typically leftovers or sandwiches that the guys get for themselves whenever they get a break in the day. You'll do the meal planning, grocery shopping, and of course, the actual cooking. You'll be the only cook for the time being, though one of our new endeavors is opening up an event space. When that gets going, we might be asked to cater, in which case, you would need to consult with the client and let me know what help you need to fulfill their wishes. Are these all things you think you'll be able to handle?"

I know it's a lot of information upfront, but really, I don't need to ask her any more questions. None of the suggestions in this LinkedIn article apply to someone who is totally underqualified, but that's ok. I already know everything I need to know about Teagan. She needs out of a bad situation, and even though it's scary for her, she's pulling up confidence from the very depths of her soul. I remember being in her shoes, sending out applications to anywhere and everywhere, praying that someone would look beyond my inexperience and give me the chance to prove myself.

"Yes!" Teagan says excitedly. "That sounds amazing. Spending all day planning meals and then getting to cook them? It's like my dream come true!"

I laugh softly at her over-the-top reaction. She might not think it's so glamorous when she has to wake up at four every morning, but I'll let her find that out on her own. Just then, I hear another noise on the other end of the line. It sounds like a banshee.

"Teagaaaaaan!" The banshee wails in the background. I swear I can *feel* Teagan tense up and crawl back into her timid little shell.

"I'm so sorry, I, um, can I call you back?" Teagan whispers.

There's a loud *thud, thud, thud* in the background and then what sounds like someone trying to twist a doorknob that's locked. "If I find you in the closet again, I'm going to throw away your dinner," the banshee woman screeches on the other side of what I assume is the closet.

"I have to go, but please just consider me for the position. I know this is so unprofessional, I swear I won't bring any drama to the ranch, I just want to work hard," she whispers even quieter now.

"You have the job, Teagan. Can I—"

"Really?!" she squeaks excitedly.

More pounding on the other side of the door makes me cringe, and I'm sure Teagan is cringing as well.

"Can I buy you a plane ticket out here?" I ask, wanting to get her away from the bitch who's screaming at her as fast as possible.

"N-no, I, uh, I have a few...obligations I need to attend to before I leave. Is that okay? I can be there in two weeks. Or I can try getting there sooner..." She trails off like she's thinking about how to rearrange her life to get here by tomorrow.

"That's fine, Teagan. Whatever works best for you. I'll email you all the details, and my offer for the plane ticket is still valid."

"Oh, that won't be necessary. It's not the money that's the issue—" Teagan gasps a little bit like she told me too much. I know better than most not to pry, so I let it go in hopes she'll trust her new family here at the ranch enough to tell us about her past one day.

"Teeeeeeeagaaaaaaaan! I will get Oscar in here to break down this fucking door! Swear to god, you're in for it this time." The banshee's tone is lower this time, more threatening.

"See you in two weeks then? We'll be in touch until then." I say, hoping to end the call on a positive note before she has to go face the terrible woman yelling at her.

"Yes, yes, thank you so much, you have no idea what this means to me," she says. I can hear her almost on the verge of tears. It makes tears spring to my eyes as well. I want to fly over to where she is and rescue her and show her people aren't all terrible. It's a lesson I've only recently learned since coming back to the ranch.

"I'll let you go, but please don't hesitate to call or text me at this number at any time for any reason, okay? We're family now."

"That's..." She sniffles and then swallows loudly. "That's very kind, thank you."

"I mean it. Are you going to be okay until you come here?"

"Yeah, yeah, of course," Teagan says. "It's...complicated. But—' She's interrupted by a louder banging on the door, and then someone growls her name. "I have to go now," she says on a shaky breath.

"Text me later, okay?"

"Okay," she whispers before hanging up.

I just want her here right now. I hate that things ended that way, but I'm thankful I can provide a way for her to get away from whatever hell she's currently in. I can't help the tears that fall down my cheeks when I think about someone hurting her or denying her food. I keep hearing her shaky voice over the phone, which only makes my gut twist up more. I'll text her in a few hours if I don't hear from her. If she doesn't answer or tells me she's in trouble, Noah and I will fly down tonight.

"Jade? What's wrong, darlin'? Phone interviews not going well?" Noah asks from the doorway of the office.

I dab away my tears and stand up, giving him a watery smile. Noah walks right up to me and pulls me into his arms. This man has held me through more tears than I thought I was capable of producing, and just like always, his cypress and rain scent, steady heartbeat, and warm, solid chest comfort me.

I finally get myself under control and step back enough to look Noah in the eyes. He cups my face and looks at me with such tender care. It's still hard to believe this sexy, sweet, cowboy is all mine. I have no idea what I did to deserve the kind of love and support he shows me every single day, but he's mine now and I'm his. That's all there is to it.

"You're killin' me, sweetheart," Noah says, dipping his head down and rubbing his nose on mine. "Why are you crying?"

"I just talked to our new cook," I finally say once I'm confident I'm not going to burst into tears again at the thought of Teagan being so far away. Noah furrows his brow in confusion. "Her name is Teagan, she's eighteen, she has no experience, and she lives half-way across the country."

Noah chuckles until he realizes I'm serious.

"I saw her application and I just..." I blow out a breath, trying to figure out how to explain it to him. "She sounded desperate. And then I called her, and she was so excited about the opportunity. But I think she's in trouble. She was hiding in a freaking closet just so she could take my call. Some awful woman was yelling at her, and I just...I could feel her fear, ya know? She needs the opportunity to get out of a bad situation, just like I did when I was her age. I know it's not the best hiring decision, and she probably won't be able to handle everything on her own right away, and with our event space opening soon, she might not—"

Noah cuts off my rant with a kiss. It's slow and sweet and grounding, exactly what I need in this moment. When we pull apart, Noah looks at me with such adoration. I'll never get tired of being precious in this man's eyes.

"I love your big heart, darlin'. Love that you want to give this girl a safe place. Love that you wanted to *make* this a safe place for anyone and everyone who walks through the front gates. I loved you when I held you in my arms that first day you were back, and I love you even more now that you'll be in my arms forever. I have loved you every moment in between, even the painful ones."

"Noah..." I whisper. "Where is all this coming from?"

"Shh, baby, you gotta let me finish," he grins, giving me a wink. The next thing I know, he's down on one knee in front of me, holding out a beautiful diamond ring. I'm too shocked to respond, so I just nod. "I've been carrying this ring around since our first kiss, just waiting for the right moment. I'm not one much for romance, but baby, you have me wanting to get everything right. I'm not usually good with my words, Jade, but you make me want to say all of the sweetest things. I want to comfort you, challenge you, laugh with you, grow with you. I want a family with you, sweetheart. I want forever with you. Will you marry me, darlin'?"

I'm a blubbering mess right now, my heart so full of love I think it might just burst. "Are you just proposing so I don't feel obligated to pay you back for all the renovations on the ranch?" I tease, tears still gathering in my eyes.

Noah stands up and slips the ring on my finger before cupping my face in his hands and tilting my head up to meet his deep, dark brown eyes. "I can think of a few creative ways you can pay me back, sweetheart," he all but growls. I open my mouth to respond, but he cuts me off again in a searing kiss. He breathes me in and swallows me down, possessing me, body and soul. I tear my mouth away from his and gulp down air, but Noah isn't finished with me yet.

I feel his lips and tongue tease up and down my neck, and then he nibbles at my pulse point, making me gasp softly. "Need to be inside you now, Jade. Need to make love to my wife," he whispers, diving in for another kiss.

I smack him playfully on the chest and take a small step back. "I haven't even said yes yet!" I say with my hands on my hips, feigning outrage.

Noah's beautiful brown eyes flash with lust, and the next thing I know, he's throwing me over his shoulder and carrying me to the bedroom. Noah claps his big, rough hand over my ass, making me squirm in his arms. "You took too long to answer," he says matter-of-factly. "Now you're mine."

We burst into the bedroom, and Noah tosses me down on the bed, making me giggle. "I don't think that's how it works," I tease him, sitting up on the bed and quirking up an eyebrow in challenge.

Noah stares right at me and starts stripping down. I watch his every move as I take my own clothes off. Soon we're both naked and staring at each other. I'll never get used to this man's perfect body. The muscles in his arms tense and tighten as he squeezes his hands into fists. My man is gloriously naked, with his massive cock growing right in front of my eyes. I lick my lips and then see a bead of precum form and drip down the head of his cock.

"Fine," Noah says with a grin, stroking his huge dick. "But we've already established that I'm a stubborn man. I'll just have to see if there are a few other ways I can get you to say yes."

I tuck my legs underneath me and get up on all fours, crawling towards him. "Maybe you just need to ask the right question," I murmur before sticking my tongue out and licking up his arousal. I never take my eyes off of his. I love seeing him get lost in his lust. Our lust.

Noah tips his head back and hisses out a breath. When he looks back down at me, I see a wild, feral glint behind his usually calm, tender gaze. Good. I love it when he loses control like this.

"What question is that?" he grits out, reaching down and tucking my hair behind my ear.

"I think you know," I whisper, licking the head of his cock again, dipping my tongue in the little slit on top, just the way he likes. I moan when he fists my hair and tugs my head back.

"Do you want to suck my fat fucking cock, darlin'?"

"God yes," I moan, licking my lips. He's still holding me tightly, my lips mere inches away from what I want most in this moment.

"Then open up, baby. I'm gonna fuck your pretty mouth now," Noah growls.

I obey his command, opening my mouth wide for him as he holds my head in place and slides his dick past my lips, stretching me wide open to accommodate his girth. I moan at his salty, earthy taste and eagerly suck more of him down until he hits the back of my throat. Noah pulls back and then enters me again, fucking my mouth nice and slowly.

I, however, don't want nice and slow. I want his passion, his dominance. Reaching out, I cup his balls in one hand and gently massage them, loving the shiver that runs through his huge, muscular body.

"Fuck," he grunts, bucking his hips more forcefully and shoving his big dick deeper into my mouth. I breathe in through my nose, relax my throat, and then dig my nails into his ass, pulling him closer to me.

Noah roars as I deep throat him. I've given Noah blowjobs before, but never like this. I was admittedly nervous, but now that he's so fucking far down my throat, I'm mad at myself that I waited to give him this pleasure.

"Jesus Christ," he growls, pumping in and out of me.

I moan around him and lick the sensitive vein on the underside of his cock with each thrust. I feel my own juices drip down my legs as my pussy throbs and aches for attention. Keeping one hand on Noah's sculpted ass, I move my other one down my body until my fingers sink into my soaking slit.

"Fuck, baby, I feel you trembling. Does giving your man pleasure make you wet?"

I answer him by moaning and bobbing my head faster, taking him deeper, digging my nails further into his skin. I'm so close, my fingers rubbing furious circles around my clit while I work Noah over until we're both in a frenzy of lust and ecstasy.

My muscles tighten up, Noah's dick swells and twitches in my mouth, I know we're both about to cum together.

But then Noah swears and pulls me off of his dick, pushing me back on the bed. An animalistic growl rises from deep in his chest, and then he crawls on top of me and slams his cock so deep, so fast, so roughly I cum instantly.

"Noah!" I shriek, clawing at his back trying to hang on for dear life as he fucks me through my orgasm and sucks on my neck. "Ohmygod, so good, so..." I scream again when I feel his teeth sink into my shoulder, another orgasm slamming into me violently, rocking me to my very core. My pussy pulses and grips him so tightly he's having trouble pulling himself back out of me.

"Goddamn, you're so fucking tight, baby," Noah grunts before taking my lips in a wild, vicious kiss. He bites my bottom lip and sucks my tongue into his mouth, devouring every inch of me. "Give me another one, darlin', need to watch you cum again."

I shake my head no, even as my hips buck and my back bows off of the bed. "I...can't..." I whimper.

"Yes, you can, and you will. Again and again. Swear to Christ, Jade, I'm going to fuck this little pussy till we're both too exhausted to move. So cum for me like the good girl you are, Jade."

I shiver at his dirty words and dirtier promises. Noah just grins wickedly at me. Then, he sits back on his heels and grabs my hips, using my body to jerk himself off. God, it's so hot the way he's moving me up and down his cock, splitting me open with each brutal thrust.

Noah tilts my hips and digs his fingers in, hard enough to bruise. A soft growl falls from my lips at the thought of him marking me. He picks up his pace, hammering into my G-spot at this new angle. My whole body convulses each time he hits the end of me.

It doesn't take much to send me flying over the edge again. My orgasm burns through me rapidly, stealing the air from my lungs as I thrash around on the bed. Noah holds my body tightly against his, feeling me cum around his dick.

My pussy is still throbbing when he pulls out and flips me over on my stomach. I get up on all fours, still trembling from my orgasm, and look at him over my shoulder. He thrusts inside of me, fucking me right. Noah slaps my ass, his big cock slamming into me, making me work for it. I move back along him, bucking my ass and panting as his powerful strokes rattle me to my very bones.

I toss my hair to one side as I look over my shoulder at him. He just smirks at me, his ripped body tense. I can feel the sweat rolling down my skin as he works me, pleasure flooding me from every direction. I feel totally mindless, absolutely devastated by his cock, but loving every single inch of it.

He slides out, making me gasp, and rolls me back over. He spreads my legs wide and pushes himself inside of me. His hands cup my breasts as he fucks me and I lean forward, kissing him as he roughly grinds his cock into my pussy. He fucks me like that, legs spread wide, mouth against my own. It feels so fucking good to have him deep between my legs. He grinds into me, fucking me hard, making me moan, making me say his name as I cream all over his thick dick.

My pussy feels raw and so, so sensitive. I can feel every ridge and vein in his cock as he pounds into me again and again. I feel liquid fire shoot through my body, singing my nerves and burning me up from the inside out.

I cling to Noah, my ankles locking behind his back, my arms clutching and clawing at his shoulders, my face buried in the side of his neck as I brace myself for the raging inferno he's calling forth from deep within my core.

"Noah," I gasp, almost afraid of what's going to happen when I finally climax.

"I've got you, sweetheart," he assures me. "Just trust me and let go, Jade. Let go for me."

All of the muscles in my body squeeze up tightly as I curl up into Noah, and then my whole world burns to the ground as I scream out my orgasm. Noah roars and sinks so fucking deep inside of me as his own release ravages his massive, muscled body. We cry out together and hold on to each other as we both fall into the very depths of pleasure.

After an eternity of intense, sharp ecstasy, I finally open my eyes. Noah is lying on his side next to me, drawing a line with his fingertips from my sternum to my belly button and back again.

"There you are," he whispers, nuzzling into my neck and kissing me there. "How do you feel, baby? Are you okay?"

I inhale a shaky breath and try to get my heart to stop thrashing around in my chest. Noah continues to drift his fingers over my skin, his touch bringing me back down to reality.

"Breathe for me, darlin'," he says gently, pressing his lips to my temple. "That's it. Good girl."

With my breathing and heart rate finally under control, I turn my head towards Noah and take in his warm brown eyes, strong jaw with the perfect amount of sexy stubble, and his soft lips pulling up into a gentle smile.

I return his smile and bite my bottom lip. Noah grasps my chin in between his thumb and forefinger, gently tugging my lip from the grasp of my teeth so he can kiss me. It's slow and tender like we have a lifetime of moments just like this. As if reading my thoughts, Noah pulls back and rubs his nose up and down mine.

"What do you say, sweetheart? Are you ready to spend forever with me?"

Tears immediately spring into my eyes as I smile with all the love and gratitude I have in my heart. I nod my head vigorously, my smile growing bigger by the second.

"I'm gonna need to hear you say it, love," Noah grins at me.

"Yes! Yes, I'll marry you!" The words are barely out of my mouth before Noah crashes his lips down on mine.

When we break apart, he chuckles and rolls onto his back, tucking me into his side. "Good to know I can get you to say yes to pretty much anything after giving you four orgasms."

I roll my eyes playfully, which makes Noah bend down and kiss my eyelids. I sigh and snuggle up closer to him, letting my fingers roam over the hard muscles in his chest and abs.

"Noah... I don't even know how to start telling you how much I love you. How much you mean to me. From the very second we reconnected, you have been my anchor. My safety. My home. I wouldn't have survived these last few months without you, and I know I wouldn't survive even a single day without you in my future. So yes, I will marry you. Yes, I'll be your forever. Yes, I'll give you all the babies you can handle," I promise, looking up at him. I'm blown away by the unshed tears glistening in his eyes. I know I will love this man more with every breath I take, until my dying day. He cups my face and draws me up for another tender kiss. I grin at him when he pulls away from me. "The orgasms aren't so bad either," I wink at him.

Noah growls and flips me on my back as he hovers over me, caging me in with a fist on either side of my head. His eyes flash with a fierce lust, but when he dips his head down, he only grazes the tip of his nose against mine, breathing me in.

"I love you so fucking much, Jade. I promise to cherish you, worship you, and protect you with everything I have. All of me is yours, sweetheart."

I'm about to open my mouth and tell him all of me is his too, but my phone chimes with an incoming text. Remembering Teagan, I twist out of Noah's arms, but turn and give him a kiss on the cheek when I see him pout.

I dig in my discarded jeans pocket for my phone and breathe a sigh of relief when I see the text from Teagan.

Teagan: Jade, thank you so much for hiring me. I was able to work out all of the details of my departure and will be at Rivera Ranch in two weeks. I'm excited to meet you in person!

I type back a quick response and then toss my phone on top of my jeans and curl back up into Noah's side, resting my head on his shoulder while my hand splays out over his solid chest.

"Looks like our cook is going to be here in two weeks," I tell him. He smiles broadly at me, a hint of mischief in his eyes.

"That sounds like just enough time to plan a wedding and break in our new event space, don't you think?"

"You want to get married in two weeks?!" I ask incredulously.

"No, I want to get married right this goddamn second, but I'm trying to be patient. I want our wedding day to be special, meaningful, and perfect."

"Oh, and you think I'll be able to achieve perfection in two weeks?" I say sarcastically.

"I think that you, my sweet, sexy, feisty little Jade, can do any goddamn thing you set your mind to," he winks at me. "I also think you underestimate what the guys and I can accomplish."

This makes me laugh. "Yeah? Jacob and Isaiah are going to decorate the barn with flowers and lace? And Cory and Zane are going to make table centerpieces with me?" I tease.

"Sweetheart, those men are among the most loyal I've ever come across, and you have had their devotion since day one. I'm pretty sure Jacob would be your maid of honor if you asked him," he chuckles. I shake my head and roll my eyes again, but I can't hide my smile. "Is that a yes then, darlin'?"

"Two weeks is crazy fast!" I protest, though there's no conviction behind it.

Noah slowly ghosts his fingertips down my spine and then grips my ass, making me gasp in surprise and desire.

"Did you already forget that I have my ways of making you agreeable?" His voice is low and gravelly, sending a shiver through my body.

"I need rest and sustenance before you make me cum so hard again!" I giggle, reaching behind me and swatting his hand away. "How about I agree right now and then you can give me those orgasms later tonight?"

Noah chuckles and wraps his arms around me. "Okay, okay, fine, I'll marry you in two weeks and give you at least four orgasms a day until then. Expect more after we're married. You drive a hard bargain, my love, but I'll do anything to make you happy."

I try unsuccessfully to suppress my smile, which only makes Noah grin even more.

We stay wrapped up in each other, talking about the wedding, the ranch, and the rest of our lives until we both drift off to sleep. The last thing I remember is breathing in Noah's cypress and rain scent and hearing his steady heartbeat. An overwhelming peace washes over me knowing I'll get to go to sleep like this every night for the rest of my life.

Epilogue

I don't know what Jade was worried about. The ceremony was perfect; small, simple, meaningful, and intimate. Now we're at the reception, which the whole town was invited to. It worked out well, not only so that Jade could see the people who once scoffed at her actually welcome her back with genuine smiles, but also because it's the official grand opening of our venue and event planning part of the ranch. Since Jade was in charge of everything, of course, it's a huge success all around.

I'm making the rounds, shaking hands and thanking our guests for attending. Jade went to find Teagan, who just flew in a few days ago. Jade has been worried that this would be too much for her to handle after only being here for a few days, but honestly, it wouldn't have mattered if the food sucked. This is the beginning of the rest of our lives together, and the only thing I need to be happy is Jade by my side.

Luckily, though, Teagan is a great chef, and she even blew our minds with the three-tiered cake she made and decorated. There's no doubt the timid, skinny girl has been through some shit, but even in the forty-eight hours she's been here, I've seen her come out of her shell more and more, especially around Jade. It makes me so proud to have such a kind, generous wife.

"I was starting to think we'd both be bachelors for life," my good friend, Knox says, pulling me back into the moment.

I chuckle and shake his hand. "It's good to see you, Knox. Taking some time off of the rodeo circuit?"

"I'm not a young man anymore," he sighs. "I have one last ride in a few weeks. Then I'm done."

"Wow, career change, then, huh?"

"Yeah, I might come work for you and Jade," he jokes.

"Or maybe you can get yourself a wife," I laugh. I expect him to scoff or give me some line about *no one can tame this bull,* but to my surprise, he clears his throat and won't meet my gaze. "Or perhaps you're already planning to be the next one down the aisle?"

He rubs the back of his neck in a nervous gesture and then finally looks up at me. I wouldn't believe it if I weren't seeing it with my own eyes, but the famous bull rider, Knox Bratton, is blushing.

"Actually, I, uh..." He clears his throat again. "Who's the new cook?"

I'm sure I look like a cartoon character with my eyes bulging out in shock. I quickly recover, though. I've known Knox for decades, and I've never seen him act like this. He looks desperate and awestruck, with an edge of possession and protectiveness. I can relate. That's exactly how I felt the first time I saw Jade when she came back to town. Those feelings have only grown more intense.

"Her name is Teagan," I say, treading lightly. I can already see the obsession, the determination setting in. Knox is a great guy, maybe a little reckless at times, but not towards other people, and never towards a woman. Still, I also feel protective over Teagan.

"Teagan," he repeats softly to himself. Shit, he's already in love with her.

"Listen, Knox. She's new here. Barely eighteen." Knox's eyes go wide at hearing that he's nearly twice her age, but then he seems to accept this information, effectively dismissing any issues he or anyone else might have about it. "I don't know her story yet, none of us really do. But just... be careful."

His eyes snap to mine, a fierce protectiveness springing to life. I've never known him to act this way about anyone before. "What do you mean? Is she in trouble? Does she need money? I have more than enough."

I see him practically vibrating with the need to fix whatever the problem is. His eyes dart around the space, no doubt trying to locate Teagan so he can offer her his kingdom.

"No, nothing like that. Jade got the sense when she did the phone interview with her that Teagan needed out of a bad situation. I don't know anything more than that, except that she's shy and a little skittish."

Knox's jaw is tense as he takes in my words. He grunts in acknowledgment as he looks over my shoulder for Teagan. I can tell the instant he sees her because his whole demeanor changes. He's softer. Gentler. And so far fucking gone for her already.

"All I'm saying, Knox, is to take your time. If you go after her with all this intensity that's coming off of you in waves, you're going to send her runnin' back to L.A."

He finally looks at me again. "What the fuck was someone as precious as her doing in L.A.? That's no place for Teagan."

"See? This is exactly what I'm talking about. You're so intense. You've always been that way, you're either all in or all out."

"I'm all fucking in, Noah," he grunts.

"I know, I know you are. I'm just saying—"

"Be careful. Got it. You better get back to your wife while I go *take my time* winning mine over."

I chuckle and pat him on the back, then turn around to survey the room for my beautiful bride. I spot her in the corner talking to Teagan, of course.

Jade looks over her shoulder at that exact moment, like she could feel my eyes on her. She breaks out into a huge smile, something she hasn't stopped doing since I proposed. She gives Teagan a hug and then makes her way through the crowd until she's standing right in front of me.

I grab her hand and kiss her palm before spinning her around in my arms and guiding my sweet Jade out to where the band is playing. She sighs happily and rests her head on my chest while we sway back and forth.

"Have I told you how unbelievably gorgeous you are today?" I murmur into the top of her head before nuzzling her hair. She left it down in wild, red waves, which I love.

"Hmm...only about five-hundred times," she laughs.

"That's all? I better up my game then, darlin'."

Jade looks up at me and smiles so sweetly. Fuck, she's so perfect. So beautiful. So *mine*.

"Tell me about the future again," she whispers, resting her head back down on my chest while I tighten my hold on her. Ever since I proposed, we've been talking about all the things we want to do with the ranch, the places we want to travel, and all the things we want our lives to look like. Every night for the past two weeks, Jade asks me to recap all of our hopes and dreams while she goes to sleep. I usually add a few plans every time, just waiting to see if she'll call me out on it.

I take a deep breath of her peaches and cream scent and close my eyes while we rock back and forth to the music.

"First, love, we're going to spend the next week in bed." This earns me a soft little laugh from my wife. "Then, once things are running smoothly here, we're going to go on a real honeymoon to Hawaii. If I haven't gotten you pregnant by the time we get back, we'll just have to spend another week in bed."

Jade laughs again and tips her head up to look at me. I swear she's glowing. She's so ethereal in this moment, her green eyes sparkling with pure delight.

"And how many kids do you want?"

"At least a baker's dozen," I tell her with a straight face. Her eyebrows jump up to her forehead, but then she gets a huge grin on her face.

Jade loops her arms around my neck and pulls me down so she can rub her nose on mine. "How about we start with the one I'm already growin' in my belly?"

I stop swaying to the music, stop breathing, stop thinking anything at all except for what my wife just told me. I blink my eyes a few times, which seems to jumpstart my heart. Cupping her face, I press my lips into hers and just rest them there, savoring this closeness, this private moment even amongst the craziness of our wedding.

"We're having a kid," I finally say. Jade smiles brightly and nods, tears gathering in the corners of her eyes. I kiss her tears away and then swing her up into my arms, spinning her around. Jade protests, though she's giggling the whole time. Finally, I slide her down my body and kiss her with everything in me. She returns my kiss with all of the love in her heart.

We're still catching our breath when Jade gets up on her tiptoes, brushing her soft lips to the shell of my ear. "Is it rude to leave our own wedding early? I need to have you inside of me right this second."

I growl softly and then kiss my wife more passionately, border lining on obscene. Before she can say another word that would have my dick busting through my pants, I scoop her up in my arms and carry her to the doorway. She laughs and kicks her feet out, looking up at me like I'm her hero. I'll never get tired of that look.

I turn around once we get to the doorway and whistle loudly so everyone looks over at us, even though most of them were already eyeing us up with knowing smiles while we were on the dance floor.

"We want to thank everyone for coming out to celebrate with us. My wife and I have some urgent business to take care of, but feel free to stick around and drink and eat to your heart's delight."

Jade is blushing, but she manages a wave before I turn back around and sprint towards the house. Jade shrieks and laughs and holds on to me with all her might.

I stop just before the threshold of our house. Even though we've been living together for months, this is still a big milestone. I look down at Jade, all of the words I want to say somehow stuck in my throat.

"I can't believe you did that," she giggles, burying her face into the side of my neck. "Now they're all going to know what we're up to!"

I bark out a laugh and kiss her on the nose. "Baby, I'm pretty sure they were going to figure it out eventually when you have my kid," I tease. "Plus, we already put on quite a show for them on the dance floor."

Jade barely contains her grin, and I can't help it, I have to kiss her again. Shifting Jade a little bit in my arms, I turn the doorknob and look my bride right in her beautiful eyes.

"Are you ready for the rest of our lives, darlin'?"

Jade bites her bottom lip and smiles, nodding her head up and down. "I can't wait for our happily ever after," she whispers.

"It starts right now, Jade," I smile down at her. "This is our happily ever after."

Also by Cameron Hart

Check out my other popular series and books!
Mafia, MC, & Bodyguard Romance:
Moscatelli Crime Family Series[1]
Di Salvo Crime Family Series[2]
Chaos MC series[3]
Savage Ride[4]
Mountain Man Romance:
Men of Blackthorne Mountain Series[5]
Bear's Tooth Mountain Men Series[6]
Cowboy & Small Town Romance:
Roped in by Love Series[7]

1. https://books2read.com/u/mqBaze

2. https://books2read.com/u/m0odzW

3. https://books2read.com/u/bMVAOk

4. https://books2read.com/u/bMVlG7

5. https://books2read.com/u/3RYDvB

6. https://books2read.com/u/mVel7A

7. https://books2read.com/u/3RYlBY